Anna Jane Buckland

Life of Hannah More

A lady of two centuries

Anna Jane Buckland

Life of Hannah More
A lady of two centuries

ISBN/EAN: 9783337114619

Printed in Europe, USA, Canada, Australia, Japan

Cover: Foto ©Raphael Reischuk / pixelio.de

More available books at **www.hansebooks.com**

HANNAH MORE IN EARLY LIFE.
(*From a picture by Opie.*)

THE

LIFE OF HANNAH MORE.

A Lady of Two Centuries.

BY

ANNA J. BUCKLAND,

AUTHOR OF
'HOMELY HEROES AND HEROINES,' 'VIOLET FLETCHER'S HOME WORK,'
ETC.

LONDON:
THE RELIGIOUS TRACT SOCIETY,
56, PATERNOSTER ROW, 65, ST. PAUL'S CHURCHYARD,
AND 164, PICCADILLY.

CONTENTS.

HANNAH MORE IN LATER LIFE.

THE LIFE OF HANNAH MORE.

CHAPTER I.

A HUNDRED AND FORTY YEARS AGO.

IT is not often that a single lifetime gathers into it the spirit of two distinct ages—of the old things which are passing away, and of the new things springing into life ; nor do we often find in one individual the type of character which clings with reverence to the past and its traditions, combined with hearty sympathy and earnest working in the struggles of the world towards a fuller day. It is only in a nature of rarely delicate balance that reverence and zeal, modesty and courage, good sense and imagination, prudence and hope, are thus equally mingled, and produce a life which is at the same time an impulse to the truer tendencies of the age and a check upon the false.

In Mrs. Hannah More, however, we may find this rare union. She was a woman of two centuries: 'In the twilight of the old and in the dawn of the new era, Mrs. More accomplished her date here,' writes her early biographer; and the value of the study of her life and work lies in the example given of a woman true to those deep essential principles which are the same in every age, and which must always lie at the heart of all woman's work, while at the same time she felt with the quick sympathy of a woman the new life that was coming in, and adapted herself to its new necessities.

The lifetime of Mrs. Hannah More extended from 1745 to 1833. Already at her birth those elements of change which broke up the cold, narrow rigidity of the eighteenth century, and ushered in the greater liberty of thought and action, the fuller life, the wider sympathies, and the deeper religious earnestness of the nineteenth century, were in existence. Abroad, Voltaire was questioning all that rested on authority alone with reckless indiscrimination; Rousseau was protesting against the despotism of conventionalism with an excess that excluded the true rule of duty. At home, Wesley and Whitfield were stirring the hearts of many into religious life by their free preaching of Jesus Christ as the hope and salvation of the human race, irrespective of ecclesiastical forms, and in spite of ecclesiastical prohibitions; in 1745 Howard began his first tour for the inspection of the prisons of England, wakening men to the idea that even the worst and most degraded of their fellow-beings had a claim on their sympathy and help.

But while these influences were already in existence at the time of Hannah More's birth, the world into which she entered had been as yet but little stirred or changed by them, and the following description from Green's ' Short History of the English People ' will fairly represent the England of 1745 : ' Never had religion seemed at a lower ebb. The progress of free inquiry, the aversion from theological strife which had been left by the Civil War, the new intellectual and material channels opened to human energy, had produced a general indifference to the great questions of religious speculation which occupied an earlier age. A large number of prelates were mere Whig partisans, with no higher aim than that of promotion. The system of pluralities turned the wealthier and more learned of the priesthood into absentees, while the bulk of them were indolent, poor, and without social consideration. The decay of the great Dissenting bodies went hand-in-hand with that of the Church, and during the early part of the century the Nonconformists declined in number as in energy. In the higher circles " everyone laughs," says Montesquieu on his visit to England, " if one talks of religion." Of the prominent statesmen of the time the greater part were unbelievers in any form of Christianity, and distinguished for the grossness and immorality of their lives. At the other end of the social scale lay the masses of the poor. They were ignorant and brutal to a degree which it is hard to conceive. For the vast increase of population which followed on the growth of towns and the development of manufactures had been met by no effort for their religious or educational improvement. Not a single new parish had been created.

Hardly one new church had been built. Schools there were none, save the grammar-schools of Edward and Elizabeth. The rural peasantry, who were fast being reduced to pauperism by the abuse of the poor-laws, were left without moral or religious training of any sort. " We saw but one Bible in the parish of Cheddar," said Hannah More later, "and that was used to prop a flower-pot." Within the towns things were worse. There was no effective police; and in great outbreaks the mob of London or Birmingham burnt houses, flung open prisons, and sacked and pillaged at their will. The criminal class gathered boldness and numbers in the face of ruthless laws which only testified to the terror of society, laws which made it a capital crime to cut down a cherry-tree, and which hung up twenty young thieves of a morning in front of Newgate ; while the introduction of gin gave a new impetus to drunkenness. In the streets of London gin-shops invited every passer-by to get drunk for a penny, or dead drunk for twopence.'

The literary world, with which Hannah More was early brought into relation, was still suffering from the paralyzing effects of the French influence introduced a century earlier. Under this influence certain fixed rules were laid down for the style, form, size, and arrangement of all kinds of literary work ; and so arbitrary was the government of these rules, that anything produced independently of them would have laid itself open to criticism as barbarous and out of taste. Another effect was to Latinize the style of English writing in its construction, rhythm, and vocabulary; so that literary expression became almost a different language from the common English speech. There was both a 'poetic diction' and a 'prose diction,' neither of which condescended to the use of those words in which the English people had since the time of Shakespeare and the translation of the Bible expressed their true mind and feelings in daily life.

The natural result of this was to narrow the circle of readers into a group of patrons and critics : for these the authors wrote ; and the higher aims of literature were sunk in the effort to flatter a patron, to win the fugitive applause of a clique, or to satisfy a superficial criticism founded on French rules, and applied only to outside form. The object of literature being thus the amusement of an idle and artificial circle, the choice of subjects often did not rise above the follies and fashions of the day, personal attacks in satires, rhyming epistles, epigrams, descriptions of Nature, taken evidently from books, and betraying little real acquaintance with her true aspects ; while through the whole ran frequent allusions, comprehensible only to those mixing in the same world as the authors.

It will be easily seen that the mighty influence of literature as the faithful representation of human character and life over the people was lost, and that it no longer could do its work in elevating them by setting before them true and possible, though higher and fairer, ideals. But already there was the dawn of a better day, a dawn which had been heralded by some rays of a truer light. Defoe had made fiction a representation of real life, and had exalted to a hero a sailor, struggling for the necessities of life on a desert island, trusting in God, and doing his duty simply and steadfastly ; and he had written his story in the common speech of the people, so that even the poorest might read and understand. And the very year before Hannah More was born Richardson had brought out ' Pamela ; or, Virtue Rewarded,' choosing for his heroine a poor servant-girl, and endeavouring to teach the poor, after his own fashion and way of looking at things, that it answered better in the end to be steadfast to the right than to yield to evil. Others there were who were beginning to feel that literature was not a mere fashionable art, exercised for the pleasure and amusement of a circle, but that it had a far higher purpose in bringing the hearts and minds of the people into contact with truth and beauty.

In following the life and literary work of Mrs. Hannah More, we shall see how she passed from the narrow view of literature prevailing in the circle of fashionable society, into sympathy with the deeper and more earnest spirit which more and more stirred the heart of the age, and wakened a wider love and concern for the interest of others. We shall also find that while she brought her literary ability into the service of God and of her fellow-creatures, she could not part with many of the old traditions as to the form and style of literary composition ; but when we think of her as the friend and favourite of Dr. Johnson in her youth, we can readily believe that while she held fast to the large-hearted care for the poor and distressed, something of which she may have learned from him, she would find it difficult to drop those phrases and the Latinized style which he had held to be necessary to the dignity of a writer.

In the literary world, at the time when Hannah More was born, there was the force of the old French *régime*, existing side by side with newly awakened thought and life. Pope was still dominant, though not living, having died the year before ; Johnson was writing, and struggling to make literary work the means of an honest, honourable livelihood. Thomson had published his ' Seasons ' not long before, in which he drew from Nature herself, and not from second-hand description Chesterfield was writing his ' Letters ' to his son.   Collins was writing his 'Odes,' and Gray his earlier poems.   Hume had just published his ' Essays, Moral, Religious, and Political.' Richardson and Fielding had each brought out his first novel the year before.   Horace Walpole had entered Parliament, and begun to exercise the sway he so long maintained over literature and society.   Garrick was acting and writing plays. Sterne was a prebendary in York Minster, preparing for writing.   Goldsmith was being educated, and Cowper was a sensitive, suffering boy at Westminster School.

CHAPTER II.

In the year 1745 there was a foundation school in the parish of Stapleton, near Bristol, the head-master of which was Mr. Jacob More. Some years before, he had come thither out of Norfolk, having been obliged, through the loss of a lawsuit, to give up his intention of entering the Church, and accept instead the office of schoolmaster. Originally the family of the Mores had been staunch Presbyterians, and two great-uncles of Jacob More had been captains of Cromwell's Ironsides; Mr. More's mother, also, used to tell how her father had protected a proscribed minister in his house, and how meetings for prayer and the preaching of God's Word were held there at midnight, to which the good people of the neighbourhood would creep stealthily through the snow, while the sturdy Puritan himself guarded his house-door with a drawn sword in his hand. Soon after Jacob More came to Stapleton he married a young woman, the daughter of a farmer; she had received a good plain education, and possessed an unusually vigorous intellect and great soundness of judgment.

Mr. and Mrs. Jacob More had already three daughters—Mary, Betty, and Sally—when in 1745 Hannah was born;

and there was afterwards another daughter, Patty. These five sisters lived together, as we shall find, in unbroken companionship and love for upwards of fifty years.

The little girls were taught to read by their mother; but their opportunities for learning must have been extremely meagre, for their father, on his way from Norfolk to Stapleton, had the misfortune to lose all his books, excepting a few Latin, Greek, and mathematical works; and it does not appear that he ever had been able to replace them. Fortunately, however, he was able to relate from memory stories from Greek and Roman history, and to repeat many of the sayings of Plutarch; and he thus supplied to his little girls the place of the books themselves. Indeed, when we recollect what the school histories of that time were, we may conclude that the loss of the books was more than compensated by the histories told by the father to his little girls gathered round his knees. In these Hannah More took the greatest delight, as she did also in the stories told by their nurse about the poet Dryden, in whose family she had lived.

Mr. More soon perceived that Hannah possessed unusual powers of mind, and he began to teach her Latin and mathematics; but she got on so much more quickly than Mr. More's pupils in the foundation school that he became alarmed; for he felt that, as these studies were at that time unusual as a part of a girl's education, there was a danger that the singularity might inflict more injury on her character than the studies themselves would benefit her mind. They were therefore dropped.

The income which Mr. More derived from the foundation school at Stapleton was probably very small. As Miss Sally afterwards told Dr. Johnson, 'We were born with more desires than guineas ; and as years increased our appetites, the cupboard at home began to grow too small to gratify them.' The father and mother, with a good sense rare at the time, determined that instead of cramping the desires of their gifted daughters, they would enable them to obtain the means for themselves of gratifying them. They should, like their father, keep a school ; and in order to fit them for this, Miss More was sent as weekly boarder to a French school in Bristol. On her return home at the end of each week, she taught her sisters all she learned ; and at length, Miss More being nearly twenty-one, the parents took a good house for their daughters in Bristol, and they opened a boarding-school for young ladies.

All the sisters seem to have been distinguished for good sense, discretion, and intelligence ; they quickly obtained pupils, and won for themselves that respect and esteem which they held through life. The school was from its commencement a success, and continued so for two-and-thirty years, when the Misses More retired with a sufficient income. Hannah More was only twelve years old in 1757, when her sisters began the school, and she and her younger sister Patty entered it as pupils. Here Hannah received all the educational advantages which could be obtained in Bristol at that time. These con- sisted chiefly in a thorough knowledge of modern languages and a fair acquaintance with English and foreign literature. She learned to speak and write French and Italian with readi- ness and correctness ; and as guineas came in to the sisters, they were able to satisfy ' their desires' by buying books. Thus Hannah early read Shakespeare, Milton, Pope, and the ' Spectator.' In the last she took great delight, an indication perhaps of that love of society, and skill in observing social characteristics and commenting on them, which she shows in her own works and letters.

She seems, also, to have early displayed that natural readiness and brilliancy in conversation which was the charm of her latter life, and the secret of much of her influence; for when during an illness she was attended by Dr. Woodward, a man of some eminence and taste, he forgot, in the attraction of her conversation, the real purpose of his visit, and after he had left her room exclaimed, ' Bless me ! I forgot to ask the girl how she is to-day.'

She had also been conscious, in quite early childhood, of the impulse to write, and her greatest delight had been to scribble little poems and essays on every bit of paper she could find, looking forward to the time, as to the realization of a golden dream, when she might be rich enough to possess a whole quire of paper. When she was sixteen years old, the elder Sheridan came to Bristol to give some lectures on eloquence. These so kindled her imagination and roused her girlish enthusiasm, that she addressed to him, after the fashion of the time, some verses, which were shown by a friend to the lecturer. They were probably only an imitation of the complimentary verses which, in those days, all persons who had the slight necessary skill addressed to one another on all possible occasions ; but in these Sheridan discovered sufficient originality and indication of genius, to induce him to request an introduction to the young girl, and to form a high idea of her talents. About the same time she also became acquainted with Ferguson, the astronomer, who had been lecturing in Bristol on astronomy, and who appears to have formed the same impression of Hannah More's intellectual ability and taste.

Hannah More's first literary production was written in 1762, when she was seventeen. It was written to supply a want felt by herself and her sisters of some dramatic poetry, which might be learnt and acted by their pupils. The acting of plays by young ladies in boarding-schools very generally prevailed at that time, adopted, perhaps, from the fame of the plays acted by the young ladies in the celebrated French boarding-school of St. Cyr, presided over by Madame de Maintenon ; but the same care does not appear to have always been taken in selecting plays suitable for representation by young ladies in many English schools ; and the Misses More no doubt often found it difficult to give their pupils ' this amusement in the exercise of recitation,' and yet ' avoid everything that is offensive on a young girl's lips.'

So Hannah More wrote ' The Search after Happiness : a Pastoral Drama for Young Ladies.' In it we may trace the influence of the literature of the day. There was a fashion for pastorals, as a reaction against the artificial life which was the real life of the time. Allan Ramsay had written ' The Gentle Shepherd, a Pastoral Play,' and Shenstone his ' Pastoral Ballads.' The style, also, of ' The Search after Happiness ' is laboured and artificial, with its ponderous words, fine phrases, and trite maxims. The metre, too, is the rhymed pentameter, the favourite metre of the eighteenth century. But there are in the aim and spirit of the piece a perception of the true principles of life, and a knowledge of the social characteristics of the time, which are remarkable in a girl of seventeen. Four young ladies ' of distinction,' having begun life upon false principles, fail, as the natural result, to find happiness. They set out therefore—

> 'To find that sovereign good of life—a friend,
> From whom the wholesome counsel we may gain
> How our young hearts may happiness obtain.'

They meet with Florella, a young shepherdess, who, hearing the object of their search, conducts them to Urania, an ancient shepherdess, living in a cottage with her two daughters. The young ladies of distinction find Urania discoursing to her daughters, the younger of whom remarks :

> ' With ever new delight we now attend
> The counsels of our fond maternal friend.'

Urania addresses the ladies :

> 'Tell me, ye gentle nymphs, the reason tell,
> Which brings such guests to grace my lowly cell.'

To which one of them replies :

> ''Tis Happiness we seek : oh, deign to tell
> Where the coy fugitive delights to dwell.'

On entering the cottage Euphelia speaks first, and explains how—

> ' Bred in the regal splendours of a court,
> Where pleasures dressed in every shape resort,
> I tried the power of pomp and costly glare,
> Nor e'er found room for thought or time for prayer.
> In different follies every hour I spent ;
> I shunned reflection, yet I sought content.'

The life of vanity, of which personal admiration was the aim, brought its natural results in envy and disappointment.

Cleora then relates her efforts to find happiness in the gratification of ambition :

'On daring wing my mounting spirit soared,
And Science through her boundless fields explored ;
I scorned the salique laws of pedant-schools,
Which chain our genius down by tasteless rules ;
I longed to burst these female bonds, which held
My sex in awe, by vanity impelled ;
To boast each various faculty of mind,
The graces Pope with Johnson's learning joined.
The schoolmen's systems now my mind employed,
Their crystal spheres, their atoms, and their void.
Newton and Halley all my soul inspired,
And numbers less than calculations fired ;
Descartes and Euclid shared my varying breast,
And plans and problems all my soul possessed.
I now with Locke trod metaphysic soil,
Now chased coy nature through the tracts of Boyle.
To win the wreath of fame, by Science twined,
More than the love of Science fired my mind.
I seized on Learning's superficial part,
And title-page and index got by heart.
This the chief transport I from Science drew,
That all might know how much Cleora knew.
Not love, but wonder, I aspired to raise,
And missed affection while I grasped at praise.'

Pastorella has dreamed her life away in romantic anticipations never realized, and represents the sentimental and sensational young lady of any period :—

'Left to myself to cultivate my mind,
Pernicious novels their soft entrance find.
I sickened with disgust at sober sense,
And loathed the pleasures worth and truth dispense.
I scorned the manners of the world I saw,
My guide was fiction, and romance my law.
A fancied heroine, an ideal wife,
I loathed the offices of real life.
These all were dull and tame ; I longed to prove
The generous ardours of unequal love.

> Or prince or peasant, each had charms alike,
> Some marvel still my wayward heart must strike.
> Whate'er inverted nature, custom, law,
> With joy I courted, and with transport saw;
> In the dull walk of virtue's quiet round
> No aliment my fevered fancy found,
> Each duty to perform observant still,
> But those which God and nature bade me fill.'

The fourth young lady, Laurinda, has perhaps fewer counterparts in the present day; her idea of happiness was in having nothing to do, no occupation, no responsibilities, no culture :—

> 'Till now I've slept in life's tumultuous tide,
> No principle of action for my guide.
> From ignorance my chief misfortunes flow,—
> I never wished to learn, or cared to know.
> With every folly slow-paced Time beguiled,
> In size a woman, but in soul a child.'

After the four young ladies have confessed how they have failed to find in life any true spring of happiness, Urania points out to them the mistakes which they have made. Euphelia had lived only for low aims, and only brought into action the lower part of her nature; the mind, the heart, the soul were starved, and only misery could be the result. Pastorella had lived only in her imagination and emotions; reason was dormant, and the sense of duty springing from love had no influence over her life. Laurinda's idle life could only produce *ennui;* beauty alone could not make up for the culture and active employment of every part of the being :—

> 'Beauty with reason cannot quite dispense,
> And coral lips may sure speak common sense.'

In conclusion, Urania gives to 'the four young ladies of

distinction in search of happiness' advice which, being founded
on eternal truth, bears repetition in the nineteenth century :

> ' In vain, ye fair, from place to place ye roam,
> For that true peace which must be found at home ;
> Nor change of fortune, nor of work can give
> The bliss you seek, which in the soul must live.
> Then look no more abroad, in your own breast
> Seek the true seat of happiness and rest.
> Fountain of Being ! teach us to devote
> To Thee each purpose, action, word, and thought ;
> Thy grace our hope, Thy love our only boast,
> Be all distinctions in the Christian lost !
> Be this in every state our wish alone,—
> Almighty, Wise, and Good, Thy will be done !

No doubt this little pastoral drama, acted or rather recited
(for action there is next to none) by the young ladies of the
Misses More's school, gave great satisfaction to the company
admitted to the performances, and helped to spread the fame
of Miss Hannah. She made one or two friends whose greater
knowledge and more vigorous intellects were of the highest
service to her in enlarging her views of things, and in giving
her better principles of literary criticism and taste. One of
these was a Mr. Peach of Bristol, a friend of Hume, who had
employed him in correcting his ' History.' Another was a
Dr. Langhorne of Weston-super-Mare, with whom she
carried on a clever and lively correspondence. At the same
time an acquaintance with Dean Tucker, Dr. Stonehouse, and
Dr. Ford led her to deeper thought and study of religious
and theological works.

She was also engaged during these years in translating
from the Italian, Latin, and Spanish, acquiring correctness
and grace of style in turning into English some of the odes

of Horace, and the dramas and poetry of Metastasio. The opera of 'Regulus,' by the latter author, she worked up into a play, and it was brought out at the Theatre Royal, Bath. As in great part a translation, an analysis of the piece would not convey any further illustration of Hannah More's mind and genius beyond the choice of a noble subject, and considerable skill in expression. She called the play 'The Inflexible Captive,' and the motto attached to it was—

> 'The man resolved and steady to his trust,
> Inflexible to ill, and obstinately just.'

There is sufficient indication in this of sympathy with strict adherence to the right, at whatever cost ; and this we shall see later was one of the most vigorous principles of Hannah More's life.

At the same time that Hannah More carried on her literary work she was also engaged in teaching in the school. The five sisters were now all partners in the establishment, and with the strong sense of duty and bright intelligence for which they were all distinguished, there can be no doubt that the education they gave their pupils was greatly superior to the usual course of instruction in girls' schools at that time. What the Misses More's school was we may in great measure judge from Hannah's later work on 'Female Education.' They seem to have had a distinct perception that the object of a girl's education is to develop her into the highest type of a true, intelligent, harmonious woman, fit to add a brighter glory and a sweeter charm to a woman's best life. Working for this with earnestness and good sense, they lived, as Johnson told them, ' lives to shame duchesses.'

2

CHAPTER III.

WHEN Hannah More was twenty-two an event occurred which no doubt had the effect of detaching her from the active part she had hitherto taken in the school, and helped to fix her attention more upon literature as her work in life.

There were at that time in the school two young ladies of the name of Turner; they appear to have been orphans, and were placed with the Misses More by their uncle, whose daughter was also a pupil in the school. The young ladies were to spend their holidays at the house of a cousin who lived at Belmont, in Bath. This gentleman was a man of more than forty years of age, unmarried, and of large property. He had a beautiful house, kept carriages and horses, and had some taste for poetry and art. A middle-aged lady resided with him, who was housekeeper, and who received his friends. Mr. Turner, in order to make the holidays agreeable to his young cousins, requested them to bring with them any of their companions whom they liked; and the two girls fixed on Miss Hannah and Miss Patty, their two youngest governesses, who were but little older than themselves.

The result of the visit was that Mr. Turner asked Hannah More to become his wife. The proposal was accepted, and was no doubt considered by Hannah's friends as a very good settlement for her. Arrangements were made for the marriage ; the sisters were anxious that she should be provided with everything necessary for her, as the wife of a man in Mr. Turner's position ; and their little savings were encroached upon in getting Hannah a handsome outfit. Her partnership in the school was given up, and she withdrew from all share in the daily work. The wedding-day was fixed more than once, but each time as the day drew near Mr. Turner found some excuse to postpone it.

It was evident he felt that he had made a mistake. He had been charmed with the conversation and wit of Hannah More, and had not, perhaps, sufficiently considered that a lively, clever young girl, gifted and educated beyond the majority of her sex, delighting in society, and already the centre of interest to a literary circle, was not just the kind of person to become all that he wanted, at his age, in a wife.

It does not appear that Hannah's love for him was very strong or deep ; her friends were displeased at his indifference, and by mutual consent the engagement was broken off. Mr. Turner had a high opinion of Miss Hannah More's talents and prospects of success as a writer, and he wished on the conclusion of the engagement to secure to her an annual sum of money, which might enable her to devote herself to literary pursuits, independently of the school, in which she had resigned her partnership. This proposal Hannah More at once rejected ; but Mr. Turner felt that some compensation of the kind was due to her for the trouble, expense, and loss of time which he had caused her. He therefore communicated with Dr. Stonehouse, the wise and kind friend through life of the Misses More, and he arranged to become the agent and trustee for the settlement of a part of the sum on Hannah More. She still objected to accept this, but her reluctance was at length overruled by her friends.

On Mr. Turner's death some years afterwards, he left her a thousand pounds besides, as a mark of his respect and regard for her.

It may have been, perhaps, as a diversion from the trouble and vexation which Hannah More's engagement had caused her, that she and her sister Patty paid their first visit to London. It was the fulfilment of a long-cherished dream, though it did not realize all their desires. Dr. Johnson had long been the favourite author of the Misses More, who appreciated the sound truth and goodness of his writings as much as their talent. They had often imagined the delight of seeing Dr. Johnson and hearing him talk, hidden safely themselves behind some screen all the time; and another long-cherished desire had been to see Garrick in some of Shakespeare's best characters; but neither of these wishes was realized on this occasion. 'That Idler, that Rambler, Dr. Johnson,' says Hannah, in writing to a friend, 'was out of town, so we were deprived of the felicity of seeing him.' Garrick was not well enough to play, or to see company, and had gone down to Hampton, where Hannah was afterwards to spend so many happy days. At the house of Sir Joshua Reynolds, the young ladies were introduced to 'a brilliant circle of both sexes.' They went to see Hampton Court, and called up all their English history over the rooms and the pictures; they had tickets offered them for 'The Birthnight.' 'But you will believe,' says Hannah, 'I did not much regard the loss of that, when I tell you that I visited the mansion of the tuneful Alexander; I have rambled through the immortal shades of

Twickenham; I have trodden the haunts of the swan of Thames!'

This visit to town was the beginning of an introduction to society in which Hannah More, and sometimes one or two of her sisters, met all the best and most distinguished persons of the day. A part of every year seems to have been spent by them in London, sometimes in lodgings, and sometimes at the houses of friends. Their next visit was paid in 1774, and this time Hannah was accompanied by Miss Sally More, a woman of great liveliness and humour, who afterwards wrote some of the best and most telling of the ' Cheap Repository Tracts ' for the poor. The sisters in town kept up a constant correspondence with those at home, and it is from these letters that the story of Hannah More's life at this time must be told.

A few days after their arrival, Miss Sally and Miss Hannah went to the play, and had the long-desired gratification of seeing Garrick in 'King Lear.' This was followed by an introduction to the great actor, through a mutual friend. Garrick was charmed with Hannah More's wit and bright enthusiasm, and invited the sisters to come to his house the next day, to meet Mrs. Montagu. To know this lady and to win her approval was an introduction at once to the most brilliant literary society of the period. She assembled at her house all the wits, authors, and critics of any name or pretensions to fame, and held *réunions* after the manner of some of the French queens of society. These meetings had acquired the name of the ' Blue-stocking Club,' in consequence of one of the gentlemen who attended them, Mr. Benjamin Stillingfleet, always wearing blue stockings. By degrees the term was applied to any pretenders to literature,

especially ladies, who had acquired the somewhat pedantic
tone of conversation which these meetings encouraged.
Mrs. Montagu was the authoress of a reply to Voltaire's
criticisms on Shakespeare; and although her defence of
Shakespeare had somewhat the tone of an apology, it must
not be forgotten that she ventured to maintain a true and
independent judgment of the great English dramatist at the
time when Voltaire had many more admirers than Shakespeare.

Another of the long-cherished wishes of the Misses More
was realized during this visit, by an introduction to their
favourite author, Dr. Johnson. They met him at the house
of Sir Joshua Reynolds; and he immediately accosted
Hannah by repeating a verse from a hymn for the morning,
which she had written for Sir James Stonehouse, their old
friend. A few days afterwards they paid a visit to Dr.
Johnson at his own house, which Miss Sally thus describes
in one of her letters home:

'We have paid another visit to Miss Reynolds. She had
sent to engage Dr. Percy ("Percy's Collection of Ballads,"
now you know him), who is quite a sprightly modern, instead
of a rusty antique, as I expected. He was no sooner gone
than the most amiable and obliging of women (Miss Reynolds) ordered the coach to take us to Dr. Johnson's *very
own house;* yes, Abyssinia's Johnson!—Dictionary Johnson!
—Rambler's, Idler's, and Irene's Johnson! Can you picture
to yourselves the palpitation of our hearts as we approached
his mansion? The conversation turned upon a new work of
his, just going to the press, "The Tour to the Hebrides."
Mrs. Williams, the blind poet, who lives with him, was
introduced to us. She is engaging in her manners, her

conversation lively and entertaining.* Miss Reynolds told the Doctor of all our rapturous exclamations on the road. He shook his scientific head at Hannah, and said " she was a *silly thing.*" When our visit was ended, he called for his hat, as it rained, to attend us down a very long entry to our coach, and not Rasselas could have acquitted himself more *en cavalier.* We are engaged with him at Sir Joshua's Wednesday evening. What do you think of us ?'

Johnson afterwards told Miss Reynolds how much the genuine, simple-hearted enthusiasm of the two girls had touched him.

During this visit Miss Reynolds also introduced them to Burke—'the sublime and beautiful Edmund Burke,' as Miss Sally calls him.

The next year we find Miss Sally and Miss Hannah More again in town ; and on this occasion Hannah was admitted among the 'blue-stockings' at Mrs. Montagu's. She describes the party in one of the letters to the sisters at home :

'I had yesterday the pleasure of dining in Hill Street, Berkeley Square, at a certain Mrs. Montagu's, a name not totally obscure. The party consisted of the hostess, Mrs. Carter, Dr. Johnson, Solander and Matty, Mrs. Boscawen,

---

* In Johnson's house, in Bolt Court, lived several distressed persons besides Miss Williams. She had been a friend of his wife, and during her lifetime had come to London for an operation in her eyes. It was unsuccessful ; she had no means of support, so Dr. Johnson kept her there, though he had to bribe the servant by half-a-crown a week to put up with her temper. There were besides beneath his roof, Robert Levitt, a poor, helpless surgeon ; Mrs. Dumoulin, widowed daughter of his old schoolmaster ; Miss Carmichael ; and a negro, all dependent upon him, and treated by him with the tender consideration of a friend rather than of a benefactor.

Miss Reynolds, and Sir Joshua, some other persons of high rank and less wit, and your humble servant—a party that would not have disgraced the table of Lælius or of Atticus. Mrs. Montagu received me with the most encouraging kindness : she is not only the finest genius, but the finest lady I ever saw. She lives in the highest style of magnificence ; her apartments and table are in the most splendid taste ; but what baubles are these when speaking of a Montagu ! Her form is delicate even to fragility, her countenance the most animated in the world—the sprightly vivacity of fifteen, with the judgment and experience of a Nestor. Mrs. Carter* has in her person a great deal of what the gentlemen mean when they say such a one is a "poetical lady ;" however, independently of her great talents and learning, I like her much. She has affability, kindness, and goodness, and I honour her heart even more than her talents ; but I do not like one of them better than Mrs. Boscawen ; she is at once polite, learned, judicious, and humble, and Mrs. Palk tells me her letters are not thought inferior to Mrs. Montagu's. She regretted (so did I) that so many suns could not shine at one time ; but we are to have a smaller party, where, from fewer luminaries, there may emanate a clearer, steadier, and more beneficial light. Dr. Johnson asked me how I liked the new tragedy of "Braganza." I was afraid to speak before them all, as I knew a diversity of opinion prevailed among the company. However, as I thought it a less evil to dissent from the opinion of a fellow-creature than to tell a falsity, I

* A lady distinguished for learning and goodness. She translated all the works of Epictetus now extant from the original Greek, Crousaz's 'Examen of Pope's "Essay on Man,"' and Algarotti's 'Explanation of the Newtonian Philosophy.' She was a frequent contributor to the *Gentleman's Magazine*, and had published a small volume of poems.

ventured to give my sentiments, and was satisfied with Johnson's answering, "You are right, madam." '

Another letter of Hannah More's shows that among the ladies who formed the circle at Mrs. Montagu's house there was a seriousness and a sense of the more solemn and earnest aims of life which raised them above that mere sparkle of intellectual intercourse which is only another form of frivolity. The letter is dated 'Sunday night,' and refers in its opening to some remarks made in a letter from one of her sisters about Sunday visiting, in reply to which she had said, ' I *did* think of the alarming call, "What doest thou here, Elijah ?" Perhaps you will say I ought to have thought of it again to-day when I tell you I have dined abroad ; but it is a day I reflect on without those uneasy reflections one has when one is conscious that it has been spent in trifling company. I have been at Mrs. Boscawen's. Mrs. Montagu, Mrs. Carter, Mrs. Chapone,* and myself only were admitted. We spent the time, *not as wits*, but as reasonable creatures, better characters, I trow. The conversation was cheerful but serious. I have not enjoyed an afternoon so much since I have been in town. There was much sterling sense, and they are all ladies of high character for piety, of which, however, I do not think their visiting on Sundays any proof, for though their conversation is edifying, the example is bad. For my own part, the more I see of the "honoured, famed, and great," the more I see of the littleness, the unsatisfactoriness of all created good, and that no earthly pleasure can fill up the wants of the

---

* Mrs. Chapone was one of the ladies of the Blue-stocking Club. She wrote 'Letters on the Improvement of the Mind,' which were highly commended at the time. She afterwards published 'Miscellanies in Prose and Verse.' Her writings are characterized by goodness and sense.

immortal principle within.   One need go no further than the company I have just left to be convinced that " pain is for man," and that fortune, talents and science are no exemption from the common lot.   Mrs. Montagu, eminently distinguished for wit and virtue—" the wisest where all are wise "—is hastening to insensible decay by a slow but sure hectic ; Mrs. Chapone has experienced the severest reverses of fortune ; and Mrs. Boscawen's life has been a continual series of afflictions.'

Miss Sally More, about the same date, tells her sisters of an evening they have spent at Sir Joshua Reynolds' with Dr. Johnson :

'Tuesday evening we drank tea at Sir Joshua's with Dr. Johnson.   Hannah is certainly a great favourite.   She was placed next to him, and they had the entire conversation to themselves.   They were both in remarkably high spirits.   It was certainly her lucky night !   I have never heard her say so many good things.   The old genius was extremely jocular, and the young one very pleasant.   You would have imagined we had been at some comedy, had you heard our peals of laughter.   They indeed tried which could " pepper the highest," and it is not clear to me that the lexicographer was really the highest seasoner.

'Yesterday Mr. Garrick called upon us.   A volume of Pope lay upon the table ; we asked him to read, and he went through the latter part of the " Essay on Man."   He was exceedingly good-humoured, and expressed himself quite delighted with our eager desire for information ; and when he had satisfied one interrogatory, said, " Now, madam, what next ?"   He read several lines we had been disputing about with regard to emphasis in many different ways before he decided which was right. He sat with us from half-past twelve till three, reading and criticizing. We have just had a call from Mr. Burke.'

Miss Sally and Miss Hannah More remained in town for six weeks, and made many new friends and acquaintances, one of the most intimate being that of the Garricks.

CHAPTER IV.

ATTEMPTS AT LITERATURE.

ONE of the results of Hannah More's introduction to the literary world, during this visit to London, was to make her feel that she ought herself to do something to render her more worthy of the companionship of the distinguished men and women with whom she had associated. On her return home, therefore, she set to work to write a poem. Among the persons to whom she had been introduced in London was Dr. Percy, who a short time before had published a collection of English ballads, 'Reliques of Ancient English Poetry.' Although Dr. Percy had somewhat altered the language of these ballads in a few cases, in order to make it conform more to the Latinized ' poetic diction ' of the time, yet the revival of the true old English literature, with its deeper and more simple feeling, and its honest, homely English language, was the beginning of the casting off of the tyranny of the French school, and its subservience to classic models and style. Hannah More possessed, as we shall see in following her life, a large amount of sound common sense ; and it was just this, and by no means the desire to be superior to her age, which made her perceive at once its prejudices and follies, and be ready to recognise the new spirit already at work, wherever this was more in accordance with truth, or better answered the higher purposes of life. She had that true independence which springs not from self-assertion, but from a strong sense of responsibility and a love of truth.

In choosing the form of her poem, Hannah More took that of a ballad, expressed for the most part in what was at that time simple English, although the critics of the period had not hesitated to speak of all the earlier English literature as 'barbarous;' and there were many who sided with Voltaire in his criticisms of 'ce bouffon d'un Shake-speare.' Hannah More's ballad was called 'Sir Eldred of the Bower.' It wants the simple, hearty feeling of the genuine ballads, such as makes them like the wild flowers in the hedges, springing up spontaneously from the very nature of the soil, and it has somewhat the air of being written to order; but it is free from the affectation of Latinized words and classical illustrations. It is a story of hasty action, under the impulse of passion :

> ' There was a young and valiant knight,
>   Sir Eldred was his name,
> And never did a worthier knight
>   The rank of knighthood claim.
>
> Where gliding Tay his streams sends forth
>   To feed the neighbouring wood,
> The ancient glory of the north,
>   Sir Eldred's castle stood.'

He was all that a knight should be — brave, generous, truthful—and resolved not to live in his father's fame, but to achieve noble deeds himself, worthy of his ancestry.

> 'Yet if the passion stormed his soul,
>   By jealousy led on,
> The fierce resentment scorned control,
>   Andbore his virtues down.'

Sir Eldred goes forth one morning, and in his wanderings comes upon a 'modest mansion' in the 'bosom of a wood,' which is inhabited by an ancient knight and his daughter:

> 'A young and beauteous dame,
>   Sole comfort of his failing years,
> And Birtha was her name.
>
> Her heart a little sacred shrine,
>   Where all their virtues meet,
> And holy hope and faith divine
>   Had claimed it for their seat.'

Near the house was Birtha's bower, planted with all her favourite shrubs and flowers:

> 'And here the virgin loved to lead
>   Her inoffensive day,
> And here she oft retired to read,
>   And oft retired to pray.',

Here Sir Eldred finds her, and overhears her morning prayer. He of course falls in love with her at first sight, and on being joined by her father (the old knight, Sir Ardolph), it is found that Sir Eldred is the son of his (Sir Ardolph's) old friend and companion-in-arms. He is invited to enter the 'modest mansion,' and he spends some days with Sir Ardolph and his daughter. He is told the story of the old knight's sorrows in the loss of his wife, and the supposed death of his son upon the field of battle. In the end Sir

Eldred asks of Sir Ardolph the hand of his daughter, to which the father promptly replies:

'"My beauteous Birtha, gracious Power,
  How could I e'er repine,"
Cries Ardolph, "since I see this hour?
  Yes, Birtha shall be thine."'

The wedding-day arrives, and after the ceremony is over:

'To recollect her scattered thought,
  And shun the noontide hour,
The lovely bride in secret sought
  The coolness of her bower.'

She remains some time absent, and Sir Eldred comes to seek her, when, to his horror, he finds her with a stranger knight, whom he imagines to have been a former love.

'Wild frenzy fires his frantic hand,
  Distracted at the sight;
He flies to where the lovers stand,
  And stabs the stranger knight.'

'Die, traitor, die!' he exclaims, and stabs the lady also, who in dying explains that it is her brother Edwy, supposed to have been killed in battle, but who has just returned to his home. The old knight has been told of his son's return, and hastens to the bower to welcome him, but sees on the ground the bodies of his son and daughter, while:

'Cold, speechless, senseless, Eldred near,
  Gazed on the deed he'd done,
Like the blank statue of Despair,
  Or Madness graved in stone.'

The effect on the father of the terrible sight is such that, falling beside them, he ' silent sunk to rest.'

A little ' moral ' is attached to the poem :

> ' The deadliest wounds with which we bleed
> Our crimes inflict alone ;
> Man's *mercies* from God's hand proceed,
> His *mis'ries* from his own.'

When Hannah More had finished her ballad, she determined to test its merits by sending it to Cadell, a publisher of some note at the time, and, like herself, a native of Stapleton. She added to it a poem which she had written some years earlier, called 'The Bleeding Rock ; or, the Metamorphosis of a Nymph into Stone.' The idea was taken from the fact of a red stream, coloured by the nature of the soil, flowing from a rock in Somersetshire, hence called the Bleeding Rock. This Hannah More supposes to be a maiden turned into stone by her own request, in order to end the misery of a life rendered hopeless through the unfaithfulness of her lover, whose vanity led him to trifle with others. Overcome with remorse, he stabs himself beside the well, from which henceforth flows the blood-red stream.

In this earlier poem all the mannerism of the time is prominent. The Somersetshire rustics are Polydore and Ianthe ; they invoke Apollo and Jove ; play upon the ' soft flute ' or ' well-strung lyre,' tuned by the Graces ; pursue with ' unerring dart the flying doe ;' and, with his poniard in his hand, ' No other nymph shall ever share my heart ; thus only I'm absolved,' cries Polydore, the English peasant, as he stabs himself. But Hannah More knew more about the condition of the Somersetshire peasantry before long, and lived to carry on so real and true a work among them, that one may fancy her smiling herself at the Polydore and Ianthe of her early days.

Mr. Cadell was much pleased with both her poems, and showed the genuineness of his approval by offering her a far larger sum than she had at all expected to receive for the right of publishing them. He added, that if she could find out what Goldsmith had been paid for 'The Deserted Village,' published five years before, he would make the sum equal to that.

Mr. Cadell had judged rightly as to the success of Hannah More's poems. Mrs. Montagu, queen of the blue-stockings, speaks of ' Sir Eldred ' in the highest terms of praise; and this vindicator of Shakespeare against Voltaire adds, ' Let me beg you, my dear madam, to allow your muse still to adorn *British* names and *British* places.' Mr. Burke thanks Hannah More for her ' truly elegant and tender performance ;' and when the sisters go up to London for their winter sojourn in town, Miss Sally writes to Miss Patty, ' From Miss Reynolds we learn that " Sir Eldred " is the theme of conversation in all polite circles, and that the " beauteous Birtha " has kindled a flame in the cold bosom of Johnson. Mr. Garrick has read " Sir Eldred " to us; and from henceforth let never man attempt to read before me if he read worse.'

Miss Hannah a few days afterwards writes, ' Dr. Johnson has invited himself to drink tea with us to-morrow, that we may read " Sir Eldred " together. I shall not tell you what he said of it, but to me the best part of his flattery was, that he repeats all the best stanzas by heart, with the energy though not with the grace of a Garrick.'

The next day Dr. Johnson went to drink tea with Miss

3

Sally and Miss Hannah in their lodgings. They spent the earlier part of the day at the Garricks', but got home by seven, before the Doctor arrived. Of this quiet evening with Johnson Miss Hannah writes : ' I hardly ever spent an evening more pleasantly or more profitably. Dr. Johnson, full of wisdom and piety, was very communicative. To enjoy Dr. Johnson perfectly one must have him to one's self, as he seldom cares to speak in mixed parties. Our tea was not over till nine o'clock; we then fell upon "Sir Eldred": he read both poems through, suggested some little alterations in the first, and did me the honour to write one whole stanza ;* but in the " Rock " he has not altered a word. Though only a tea visit, he stayed with us till twelve.'

Miss Sally sends home her account of the same evening : ' After much critical discourse, Dr. Johnson turns round to me, and with one of his most amiable looks, which must be seen to form the least idea of it, he says, " I have heard that you are engaged in the useful and honourable employment of teaching young ladies !" Upon which, with all the same ease, familiarity, and confidence we should have done had only our own dear Dr. Stonehouse been present, we entered upon the history of our birth, parentage, and education ; showing how we were born with more desires than guineas, and how as years increased our appetites the cupboard at home began to grow too small to gratify them ; and how, with a bottle of water, a bed, and a blanket, we set out to seek our fortunes ; and how we found a great house with nothing in

* ' My scorn has oft the dart repelled
  Which guileful beauty threw ;
  But goodness heard and grace beheld
  Must every heart subdue.'

it ; and how it was like to remain so, till, looking into our knowledge-boxes, we happened to find a little *learning*, a good thing when land is gone, or rather none ; and so at last by giving a little of this little *learning* to those who had less, we got a good store of gold in return ; but how, alas ! we wanted the wit to keep it. " I love you both," cries the *inamorato*— " I love you *all five*. I never was at Bristol—I will come on purpose to see you. What ! five women all live happily together ! I will come and see you—I have spent a happy evening—I am glad I came ; God for ever bless you ! you live lives to shame duchesses." He took his leave with so much warmth and tenderness, we were quite affected at his manner.'

Miss Sally More returned to Bristol to begin another half-year's work in the school, leaving Miss Hannah in town, where she remained six months living with the Garricks, partly at their London house in the Adelphi, and partly at their country residence at Hampton.

During this time she read and wrote for some hours of every day, and had the advantage of intercourse with many persons of intellect and culture. 'It is not possible,' she writes to her sisters, 'for anything on earth to be more agreeable to my taste than my present manner of living. I am so much at my ease ; have a great many hours at my own disposal to read my own books and see my own friends, and whenever I please may join the most polished and delightful society in the world. Our breakfasts are little literary societies ; there is generally company at meals, as they think it saves time by avoiding the necessity of seeing people at other seasons. Mr. Garrick sets the highest value upon his time of anyone I ever knew. From dinner to tea we laugh, chat, and talk nonsense ; the rest of his time is generally devoted to study. I detest and avoid public places more than ever, and should make a miserably bad fine lady. What most people come to London *for* would keep me *from* it.'

Whilst Hannah More was in London the monotony of the school life of the four sisters at home was broken in upon by a visit from Dr. Johnson and Boswell. Hannah's letters were, no doubt, also the means of bringing variety and liveliness into their six months of daily work. She tells them of her going to the trial of the would-be Duchess of Kingston before the House of Lords, of Sir Joshua Reynolds's new picture of the infant Samuel, about which the fashionable world are all asking, 'Who *is* Samuel ?' of a new hotel in St. James's Street, called the ' Savoir Vivre,' at which on the first occasion the rooms were used sixty thousand pounds were lost at cards ; of the death of a relative of the Duchess of Chandos at the card-table, after which the company continued their play ; and of Garrick's last performances of many of his celebrated parts previous to his retiring from the stage.

In the beginning of June Hannah More returned to Bristol, where she spent some months studying and writing, and keeping up correspondence with the Garricks, Mrs. Boscawen, and other London friends.

The next visit appears to have been into Norfolk, where she made acquaintance with many of her father's relatives, whom the Mores of Bristol had never seen before. These relatives had much of the simple hospitality and godly earnestness of their Puritan ancestors. In writing to her sisters, Hannah speaks of their intelligent study of divinity, and of their great liberality in contributing to every good object, upon which she makes the just remark, ' I have long ago found out that hardly any but plain, frugal people ever do generous things. Our cousin, Mr. Cotton, who, I dare say, is often ridiculed for his simplicity and frugality, could yet lay down two hundred pounds without being sure of ever receiving a shilling interest.'

Hannah More returned home through London, stopping at the Garricks', and with them she visited at Farnborough Place in Hampshire, where she met Dr. and Mrs. Kennicott. With them she at once formed an intimate friendship, which lasted through their lives. Hannah More's greater seriousness and more earnest views of life brought them, perhaps, into sympathy. Beneath the vivacity and ease which led her to adapt herself readily to all kinds of society, there already existed that independence of character and steadfast adherence to duty which so strongly marked her later years. A little incident occurred during this visit to Farnborough Place which illustrates this. She had always maintained the obligation of keeping holy the Sabbath, and when one Sunday it was proposed to have secular music, Garrick made the way easy to her to withdraw by saying, ' I know you are a *Sunday woman;* retire to your room, and I will call you when the music is over.' And Hannah rose and left the room.

At the same time it may not be out of place to notice here that the life she was leading at this time was one which had very little of high purpose in it. The society she mixed in, though composed of persons of more than average intellect, was brilliant rather than thoughtful ; their aims were too much centred in self-gratification ; and the mutual admiration they constantly expressed for one another tended to produce egotism and vanity, rather than sincere love of truth and reverent admiration of all that was noble and good. Hannah

More's own sympathies were narrowed by it. Her letters at this period are filled with accounts of the pleasures of the hour, the visits she pays, the great people she meets, the compliments she receives. There is a strange absence of all expression of interest in her family; she scarcely ever names her father or mother, or makes any allusion to her sisters and their work. Even her most eminent London friends, Dr. Johnson and others, from whom she had received so much kindness, are sometimes mentioned with a want of feeling which shows that frivolity had in some measure produced its usual effect upon the heart.

CHAPTER V.

DURING the time which Hannah More spent at home after her residence with the Garricks, she had been occupied in writing a play. Garrick had no doubt encouraged her to make the attempt, and it must also be borne in mind that the drama supplied at that time the kind of opportunity for testing the powers of a writer which is now afforded by the modern novel. If an author wished to try whether he were capable of stirring and interesting others by his conceptions of character and his representations of life under its rarer aspects, or as moved by the deeper emotions, he wrote a play; and then anxiously watched its reception by the public and the critics. Hannah More took as a slight foundation for her play an old French story of Raoul de Coucy ; but, faithful to Mrs. Montagu's advice, to allow her 'muse still to adorn British names and British places,' she placed the scene in the north of England, and chose for her *dramatis personæ* the old, well-known heroes of English song, Douglas and Percy. The story is an 'oft-told tale' of those thwarts and complications arising out of the feuds and the crusading life of the Middle Ages.

Elwina, the daughter of Earl Raby, was betrothed to Percy,

Earl of Northumberland; but one summer morning, while chasing the deer among the Cheviots, some of Lord Raby's knights were insulted by the herdsmen and foresters of Lord Percy. Lord Raby took the insult as an intentional offence to himself, and would receive no apology from Lord Percy. Elwina was commanded to renounce her lover, which she did, but says :

> ' Oh, 'twas a task too hard for all my duty !
> I strove and wept ; I strove—but still I loved.'

Soon afterwards she was forced into a marriage with Douglas, who is not aware that she had ever been betrothed to his rival and enemy. Lord Percy, in the meantime, has joined the Crusade, hopeless of reconciling Lord Raby, but trusting to the influence of absence and time in lessening his displeasure ; he therefore hears nothing of Elwina's marriage to Douglas.

Elwina endeavours to do her duty to her husband, but in the first scene Douglas complains that it is only

> ' Cold, ceremonious, hard, unfeeling duty.
> While duty portions out the debt it owes,
> With scrupulous precision and nice justice,
> Love never measures, but profusely gives,
> Gives like a thoughtless prodigal its all,
> And trembles then, lest it has done too little.'

He suspects that her heart is not his ; and when the news comes that the King is returning from the Crusade, and Lord Raby wishes his daughter to go to court to welcome him and his knights, Douglas surmises from her reluctance that she is attached to one of the crusading heroes.

This suspicion is confirmed when Harcourt, friend and

messenger of Earl Percy, arrives at Raby Castle, the residence of Elwina. He announces the approach of Percy, and the constancy of his love for Elwina. Douglas throws Harcourt into prison, and encounters Percy, who had unexpectedly arrived and met Elwina in the garden. A duel follows, in which Percy is killed. Earl Raby then comes upon the scene, and explains to Douglas that Percy had left England betrothed to Elwina, and had never since heard of her marriage, and that he had been guilty of forcing his daughter into it against her own will. Douglas, in remorse, stabs himself, and Elwina drinks poison. The character of Elwina is clearly and delicately conceived, and in the struggle between feeling and duty, she is throughout loyal to duty while tender in feeling.

Garrick took the greatest interest in the composition of 'Percy,' and wrote for it the prologue and the epilogue. Whilst Hannah More was engaged upon it during the summer of 1777, a brisk correspondence was carried on between her and Mr. Garrick. Some of his letters are interesting in the indication they afford that the great actor and old friend of Johnson was a man with serious views of life, and accustomed to think on those deeper truths which are the essentials of religious life.

Mr. Harris, of Covent Garden, undertook to bring out 'Percy,' and in November Hannah More went to London to be present at its first representation. She had lodgings in Gerrard Street, from which she writes to her sisters: 'It is impossible to tell you of all the kindness and friendship of the Garricks; he thinks of nothing, talks of nothing, writes of nothing, but "Percy." He is too sanguine; it will have a fall, and so I tell him.' Garrick's judgment was, however, more

correct than the author's. The play was undoubtedly a
success. At ten o'clock at night Hannah More sits down in
Mr. Garrick's study to tell the anxious sisters in Bristol of its
favourable reception. 'He puts the pen in my own hand,
and bids me say that all is just as it should be. Nothing was
ever more warmly received. I went with Mr. and Mrs. Garrick,
sat in Mr. Harris's box in a snug dark corner, and behaved
very well—that is, very quietly. The prologue and epilogue
were received with bursts of applause—so, indeed, was the
whole, as much beyond my expectation as my deserts.
Mr. Garrick's kindness has been unceasing.' After the
second night Hannah More writes again to her sisters : ' I
may now venture to tell you what I would not hazard last
night, that the reception of "Percy" exceeded my most
sanguine wishes. I am just returned from the second night,
and it was, if possible, received more favourably than on the
first. One tear is worth a thousand hands, and I had the
satisfaction to see them shed in abundance. The critics, as is
usual, met at the Bedford last night to fix the character of the
play. If I were a heroine of romance, and were writing to
my confidante, I should tell you all the fine things that were
said; but as I am a real, living Christian woman, I do
not think it would be so modest. . . . I think some of
you might contrive to make a little jaunt, if it were only
for one night, and see the bantling. Adieu, and some of
you come.'

The school half-year had not yet come to a close, but
Miss Sally and Miss Patty contrived to leave their work
and travel up to town, to enjoy one night of Hannah's
triumph. It was the twelfth night of the play, and, to the
gratification of the sisters, 'the theatre overflowed prodigiously,

notwithstanding their Majesties and the "School for Scandal" at the other house.'

' Percy' had the most successful run of all the tragedies brought out that winter, and it kept its place on the stage for three or four years afterwards, when Mrs. Siddons played Elwina. The first edition of four thousand copies was sold within a fortnight, and a second edition called for. Meanwhile congratulations and compliments poured in upon Hannah More from every side.

Something must be granted to its favourable introduction by Garrick; something, also, to the fact that Hannah More's circle of personal friends was now very large, and included most of the influential persons who, as critics and ' blues,' led the taste of a great number of others. She had by the charm of her agreeable manners and brilliant conversation become ' the fashion,' and her work was not likely, perhaps, to be submitted to the vigorous criticism and guarded applause bestowed upon an ordinary play, resting its claims for approval solely on its own merits. To this must be added Hannah More's own frank admission : ' I do not wish to rise on any-body's fall, but it has happened rather luckily for " Percy," that so many unsuccessful tragedies were brought out this winter.' But, after taking all these things into consideration, there remains the fact that not only at the time was it said to be the most successful tragedy which had appeared for many years, but that after Garrick was dead, and Hannah More had withdrawn from the world, and the old circle to which she belonged was broken up, ' Percy' still held its place in public esteem. At the time when Hannah More herself had formed such strong objections to the theatre that nothing could induce her to enter it, ' Percy' was being played with Mrs.

Siddons as Elwina, and we find that Horace Walpole and
Burke 'raved' at the authoress for refusing to go and see it.
It was translated into German, and acted in Vienna ; and
was also bespoken by M. de Calonne, who had translated it
into French, and wished to see it acted in England before
bringing it out upon the French stage.   Hannah More made
by the play between seven and eight hundred pounds.

After spending the winter in town, she returned in April to
Bristol, and spent the next few months in writing another
tragedy—'Fatal Falsehood.'   As before, Garrick was her
friend and counsellor in her work ; she had sent four of the
acts to him, and he had expressed his approval of them ; and
she had completed the fifth, when she received a sorrowful
summons from Mrs. Garrick, asking her to come to her in her
first desolation and grief at the death of her husband.   Hannah
More was ill in bed when she received Mrs. Garrick's letter,
but she rose immediately and set off for London.   On arriving
at the house where she had spent so many happy hours and
received so much kindness, she found Mrs. Garrick just
quitting it in order to go to a friend's while the painful preparations were being made for the public funeral and for the
lying in state.

'She was prepared for meeting me,' writes Hannah More to
her sisters, 'and she ran into my arms, and we both remained
silent for some minutes ; at last she whispered, " I have this
moment embraced his coffin, and you come next."   She soon
recovered herself, and said with great composure, " The
goodness of God to me is inexpressible ; I desired to die, but
it is His will that I should live ; and He has convinced me
He will not let my life be quite miserable, for He gives
astonishing strength to my body and *grace* to my heart.   I

deserve neither, but I am thankful for both." She thanked
me a thousand times for such a real act of friendship, and
bade me be comforted, for it was God's will. She told me
they had just returned from Althorpe, Lord Spencer's, where
they had reluctantly been dragged, for he had felt unwell for
some time; but during his visit he was often in such fine
spirits, that they could not believe he was ill. I can never
cease to remember with affection and gratitude so warm,
steady, and so disinterested a friend ; and I can most truly
bear this testimony to his memory, that I never witnessed in
any family more decorum, propriety, and regularity than in
his, where I never saw a card, or even met a person of his own
profession at his table, of which Mrs. Garrick, by her elegance
of taste, her correctness of manners, and very original turn of
humour, was the brightest ornament. All his pursuits and
tastes were so decidedly intellectual, that it made the society
and the conversation which were always to be found in his
circle interesting and delightful.'

Another letter describes the funeral of Garrick in Westminster
Abbey, and the return of Mrs. Garrick to their house in the
Adelphi. 'She bore it all with great tranquillity,' Hannah
More writes ; ' but what was my surprise to see her go alone
into the chamber in which he had died that day fortnight ! She
had a delight in it beyond expression. I asked her the next
day how she went through it. She told me, very well ; that
she first prayed with great composure, then went and kissed
what had so lately been his dying bed, and got into it with
a sad pleasure. Not a sigh escapes our poor friend which
she can restrain. When I expressed my surprise at her
command, she answered : "Groans and complaints are very
well for those who are to mourn but for a little while, but a

sorrow that is to last for life will not be violent and romantic." ' Hannah More spent some months with her friend Mrs. Garrick, living principally at the house at Hampton, and spending the time in retirement and study.

On their occasional visits to town she renewed in some measure her intercourse with her friends, and speaks of meeting Miss Burney, who had lately brought out her first novel, ' Evelina.'

She also visited Mrs. Delany, a lady of much social celebrity, once the friend and correspondent of Swift, but now of great age, and living a very retired life. She was still, however, greatly esteemed, and was much beloved by a large circle of friends, amongst them Queen Charlotte and the elder princesses, who frequently visited her. Through Mrs. Delany, Hannah More became acquainted with Horace Walpole, and was soon added to the list of his numerous correspondents.

On coming up to town she had brought with her her new tragedy, ' Fatal Falsehood,' intending to offer it to Mr. Harris, of Covent Garden, and to leave it in his hands until the next winter ; but, although the season was already advanced, he wished to bring it out at once ; and after some reluctance on Hannah More's part she at length consented to allow it to appear. The time was, no doubt, unfavourable, for the weather was warm, and the play had but a short run compared with ' Percy.' It was, however, well received, and the printed copies sold so well that soon a second edition was called for.

It is necessary to dwell on the success of Hannah More's plays, not on account of the worth of the work itself, but as indicating that the change in her opinions regarding theatrical amusements resulted from convictions which led her to give herself to work of a different kind, and not from the vexed feeling of a disappointed play-writer. The whole of her early life was a splendid social success; and her withdrawing from it was because she felt that it was not a true and noble life, and that, even with religious principle at heart, it could not be made so. It was the deeper and more absorbing love of God and humanity which in the end called her away from it all; but as yet she was still a woman of the eighteenth century, satisfied with the sparkling surface of society, anxious to win the admiration of a narrow clique, and indifferent to deeper questions affecting the welfare of humanity outside of her literary circle. She had learned to observe keenly, to discriminate, to criticize, and to censure; but the time was yet to come when she united these abilities with a deeper sense of responsibility to God, and a larger-hearted love to man, such as in her later life made her work one of rare service.

CHAPTER VI.

THE 'SACRED DRAMAS' AND 'SENSIBILITY.'

A CONSIDERABLE portion of the next few years of Mrs. Hannah More's life was spent in London, or at Hampton with Mrs. Garrick. During this time she made many new friends, and mixed constantly with her old ones — Mrs. Montagu, Mrs. Boscawen, Horace Walpole, Mrs. Delany, Miss Burney; but among her later acquaintances occur the names of Dr. Kennicott, Dr. Horne, afterwards Bishop of Norwich, Dean Tucker, Dr. Lowth, and Dr. Porteus, men of intellect and learning, who were directing their powers to the study of religion and the service of God rather than to the intellectual trifling which prevailed among the 'blue-stocking' set. Her letters to her sisters during this period contain the same repetition of visits and compliments, with here and there little incidents of more than present and personal interest, as indicating the state of society and the tone of opinion of the day. Such is the conversation with Dr. Johnson, who told Hannah More that George III. had urged upon him to include Spenser in his 'Lives of the Poets,' but he had not agreed to do so, for the booksellers had not named Spenser in their list of poets. On another occasion, mentioning to Dr. Johnson that she had read 'Les Pensées de Pascal,' he exclaimed, with tears in his eyes, and 'with the most affecting earnestness': 'Child, I am heartily glad you read pious books, by whomsoever they may be written.'

About this time Hannah More published her 'Sacred Dramas,' and with them a poem on 'Sensibility.' Her idea in the 'Sacred Dramas' was to turn the dramatic art to high and holy purposes, on the same principle that she afterwards wrote her religious novel 'Cœlebs.' But she did not perceive the difference between using fiction to show the practical illustration of some great and important truths, and the giving a new and different form to the simple narratives of the Bible. In the present day, when we are familiarized in the best literature with a purer Saxon-English, the attempt to put sounding words and phrases into the mouths of Scripture characters is even more offensive than in Hannah More's own time. The subjects dramatized are, 'Moses in the Bulrushes,' 'David and Goliath,' 'Belshazzar,' 'Daniel;' and there are also reflections on 'King Hezekiah in his Sickness,' such as might have been written by Johnson or any other moralist in the days of Latinized English, but which have no connection but the name with the King Hezekiah of the Bible. The 'Sacred Dramas' appear to have given pleasure to many earnest persons at the time, who longed to see so great a power as the drama used to elevate instead of to degrade ; but in regard to the purpose they were intended to serve, it is needless to say that they were failures.

The poem on 'Sensibility' had a truer design. In an age of little deep feeling it had become the fashion to affect to be moved by the most trifling appeals to the emotions. Miss Harriet Byron, the much-admired heroine of the much-read novel, 'Sir Charles Grandison,' is constantly spoken of as a

4

young lady 'of exquisite sensibility,' and her fine feelings and
tears are paraded throughout the whole nine or ten volumes of
the novel.   Goethe's 'Sorrows of Werther' had established
sensibility rather than duty as the principle of action, and
he only followed in the steps of Rousseau and Sterne.   The
false assumption of feeling and its usurpation over duty
is the subject of the first part of Hannah More's poem on
'Sensibility':

> 'While her fair triumphs swell the modish page,
> She drives the sterner virtues from the stage ;
> While Feeling boasts her ever-tearful eye,
> Fair Truth, firm Faith, and manly Justice fly.'

Then, after praise of true sensibility :

> 'She does not know thy power who boasts thy fame,
> And rounds her every period with thy name ;
> Nor she who vents her disproportioned sighs
> With pining Lesbia, when her sparrow dies ;
> Who thinks feigned sorrows all her tears deserve,
> And weeps o'er Werther while her children starve.
>
> There are who fill with brilliant plaint the page
> If a poor linnet meet the gunner's rage ;
> There are who for a dying fawn deplore
> As if friend, parent, country were no more ;
> There are whose well-sung plaints each breast inflame,
> And touch all hearts but his from whence they came.
>
> He, scorning life's low *duties* to attend,
> Writes odes on friendship, while he cheats his friend.
> Of jails and punishments he grieves to hear,
> And pensions prisoned virtue with a tear ;
> While unpaid bills his creditor presents,
> And ruined innocence his crime laments.
> O love divine, sole source of charity !
> More dear one genuine deed performed for thee

Than all the periods feeling e'er could turn,
Than all thy touching page, perverted Sterne !
One silent wish, one prayer, one soothing word,
The page of mercy shall well pleased record ;
One soul-felt sigh by powerless pity given,
Accepted incense shall ascend to heaven.

The sober comfort, all the peace which springs
From the large aggregate of little things,
On these small cares of daughter, wife, or friend
The almost sacred joys of home depend ;
There, Sensibility, thou best may'st reign,
Home is thy true legitimate domain.'

In the following lines Hannah More discriminates the
falseness of the idea, which at that time pervaded foreign
literature even more than English, that feeling in itself is the
true guide of conduct, and stands for moral principle :

'As feeling tends to good or leans to ill
It gives fresh force to *vice or principle.*
'Tis not a gift peculiar to the good,
'Tis often but the virtue of the blood,
And what would seem compassion's moral flow
Is but a circulation swift or slow ;
But to divert it to its proper course,
There wisdom's power appears, there reason's force.
If, ill directed, it pursue the wrong,
It adds new strength to what before was strong ;
But if religion's bias rule the soul,
Then sensibility exalts the whole,
Sheds its sweet sunshine on the moral part,
Nor wastes in fancy what should warm the heart.
To give immortal mind its finest tone,
O Sensibility, is all thine own.'

The poem on ' Sensibility ' was followed soon after by the
' Bas Bleu ; or, Conversation.' It was written at first for pri-

vate circulation, but quickly found its way into print, for George III. had desired to have a copy of it, and Dr. Johnson had said of it to Mrs. Thrale, 'Miss Hannah More has written a poem called the "Bas Bleu," which is in my opinion a very great performance ; it wanders about in manuscript, and surely will soon find its way to Bath.' But Hannah More had almost as little claim to be called a poet as she had to be a dramatist. She had skill in writing verse, and the 'Bas Bleu' is a clever, neat description of the parties held at the houses of Mrs. Vesey, Mrs. Montagu, and others, where conversation was the only amusement of the evening. The persons composing this brilliant circle were nearly all distinguished by talent, and they studied conversation as an art ; consequently all who speak of these assemblies testify to the brightness and wit of the social intercourse. There was also a refinement and good sense governing the conversation, which was rare in any circle at that time.

But there was little real fruit produced by this energy of intellectual life ; and soon the sparkle of it passed away, as the circle was broken in upon by the death or ill-health of many of its most shining members. This hushing into utter silence of all the wit and brilliant conversation which had so charmed Hannah More, and in which she bore no insignificant part herself, seems to have pressed upon her more deeply the thought that her talents were given her for higher service than to add to the glitter of social intercourse, that she might do some good work for those who needed it, which would endure, and 'whose glorious beauty' should not be 'a fading flower.'

Amongst those friends who were passing away was her kind old friend Dr. Johnson. He died while Hannah More was staying with Mrs. Garrick at Hampton ; and in a letter to her sister she relates the account she had received of his death from Mr. Pepys :

'A little before he died he said to his physician, "Doctor, you are a worthy man, and my friend, but I am afraid you are not a Christian. What can I do better for you than offer up in your name a prayer to the great God that you may become a Christian in my sense of the word ?" Instantly he fell on his knees and put up a fervent prayer. When he got up he caught hold of the physician's hand and cried, "Doctor, you do not say 'Amen.'" The doctor looked foolish, but, after a pause, he said "Amen." Johnson then said, "My dear doctor, believe a dying man : there is no salvation but in the sacrifice of the Lamb of God." A friend desired he would make his will ; and as Hume in his last moments had made a declaration of his opinions, he thought it might tend to counteract the effect of this if Johnson would make a public confession of his faith in his will. He said he would ; seized the pen with great earnest- ness, and asked what was the usual form of beginning a will. His friend told him. After the usual form he wrote : "I offer up my soul to the great and merciful God ; I offer it full of sin, but in full assurance that it will be cleansed in the blood of my Redeemer." And for some time he wrote on with the same vigour and spirit, as if he had been in perfect health. He talked of his death and funeral at times with great composure. On the Monday morning he fell into a sound sleep, having exclaimed just before, "Jam moriturus" (Now I am about to die). He continued in that state for twelve hours, and died without a groan. His death makes a kind of era in literature : piety and goodness will not easily find a more able defender ; and it is delightful to see him set, as it were, his dying seal to the professions of his life and to the truth of Christianity.'

Not long before the death of Dr. Johnson, Hannah More had been brought face to face with death beside the dying bed of Dr. Kennicott. On hearing of his dangerous illness she had hastened to his house in Oxford, in order to give all the comfort and help she could to Mrs. Kennicott. In a letter to her sister she says : ' My last will have prepared you to expect the contents of this letter. Dear Dr. Kennicott expired yesterday about four o'clock in the afternoon. I saw him breathe his last. I have got her away from him downstairs ; and for the last two hours ran continually up and down from the afflicted wife to the expiring husband, she all the time knowing he was in the last agonies, yet, when I came to break it to her, she bore it with the utmost fortitude. She has been very composed ever since ; indeed, she is a true Christian heroine. Thus closed a life the last thirty years of which was honourably spent in collating the Hebrew Scriptures. One now reflects with peculiar pleasure that, among other disinterested actions, he resigned a valuable living because his learned occupation would not allow him to reside upon it. What substantial comfort and satisfaction must not the testimony which our departed friend was enabled to bear to the truth of the Holy Scriptures afford to those who lean upon them as the only anchor of the soul ! When Dr. Kennicott had an audience of the King to present his work, his Majesty asked him what upon the whole had been the result of his laborious and learned investigation ; to which he replied that he had found some grammatical errors and many variations in the different texts, but not one which in the smallest degree affected any article of faith or practice.'

Then follows a sketch of Dr. Kennicott's character, which Hannah More drew up while it was fresh in her recollection, at the close of which is the following note :

' Oxford, August 21, 1783.

'This imperfect sketch of the character of an excellent man was drawn by one who affectionately esteemed him ; who two days ago heard from him the groan which could not be repeated, and who is just now going to see him laid in the grave. May the recollection of that awful scene long rescue her heart from the vanity and weakness to which it is too subject !'

CHAPTER VII.

COWSLIP GREEN.

THE desire for rest, and a feeling of the unfruitfulness of her London life, induced Hannah More to buy some land near Bristol, and build upon it a cottage, where she might live in retirement some part of every year, hoping that this 'might favour her escape from the world gradually.' The name given to the house was 'Cowslip Green,' which Walpole declared must be 'some relation, a cousin at least, to Strawberry Hill.' In this cottage, which was about ten miles from Bristol on the Exeter road, Hannah More spent some months each year, her sisters being still engaged in their school at Bristol. She seems to have had the idea that by shutting herself up in her cottage, and amusing herself with the more simple pleasures of gardening and other country occupations, she would find that happiness and satisfaction in life which she felt was missing in the days she spent among a crowd of admiring acquaintance. She discovered, however, after awhile, that the simpler pleasures of a country life, when made the sole aim of life, were as unsatisfactory as the pleasures of her social life in London.

It was after having tried the experiment of two summers passed at Cowslip Green that she writes thus to John

Newton, whose acquaintance she had made a short time before in London :

'*Cowslip Green*, 1787.

' MY DEAR SIR,

' I am really extremely obliged to you for your very agreeable and instructive letter. Whenever I receive a letter or a visit, I always feel pleased and grateful in proportion to the value I set on the time of the visitor or the writer ; and when a friend who knows how to work up to advantage all the ends and fragments of his time, is so good as to bestow a little portion of it on me, my heart owns the obligation ; and I wish it were understood as preliminary in all acquaintance, that where no good can be done and no pleasure given, it will be so unprofitable a commerce as to be hardly worth engaging in. I am sure your letter gave me pleasure, and I hope it did me good, so you see it is doubly included in the treaty.

' Excepting one month that I have passed at Bath on account of health, and occasional visits to my sisters at Bristol—in this pretty quiet cottage, which I built myself two years ago, I have spent the summer. It is about ten miles from Bristol, on the Exeter road, has a great deal of very picturesque scenery about it, and is the most perfect little hermitage that can be conceived. The care of my garden gives me employment, health, and spirits. I want to know, dear sir, if it is peculiar to myself to form ideal plans of perfect virtue, and to dream of all manner of imaginary goodness in untried circumstances, while one neglects the immediate duties of one's actual situation ? Do I make myself understood ? I have always fancied that if I could secure to myself such a quiet retreat as I have now really accomplished, that I should be wonderfully good ; that I should have leisure to store my mind with such and such maxims of wisdom ; that I should be safe from such and such temptations ; that, in short, my whole summers would be smooth periods of peace and goodness. Now the misfortune is, I have actually found a great deal of the comfort I expected, but without any of the concomitant virtues. I am certainly happier here than in the agitation of the world, but I do not find that I am one bit better : with full *leisure* to rectify my heart and affections, the disposition unluckily does not come. I have the mortification to find that petty and (as they are called) innocent employments, can detain my heart from heaven as much as tumultuous pleasures. If to the pure all things are pure, the reverse must be also true when I can contrive to make so harmless an employment as the cultivation of flowers stand in the room of a vice, by the great portion of time I give up to it, and by the entire dominion it has over my mind. You will tell me that if the affections be estranged from their proper object, it signifies not much whether a bunch of roses or a pack of cards effects it. I pass my life in intending to get the better of this, but life is passing away, and the reform never begins. It is a very significant saying, though a very old one, of one of the Puritans, that " Hell is paved with good intentions." I sometimes tremble to think how large a square my procrastination alone may furnish to this tesselated pavement.

' I shall come London-ward next month, but shall be only geographically nearer you, as I pass much of the winter at Hampton. I shall gladly seize every opportunity of cultivating your friendship, and must still regret that your house and the Adelphi are so wide of each other. I heartily commend myself to your prayers, and am with the most cordial esteem, dear sir, your much obliged and faithful,

'H. MORE.'

In reply to this John Newton writes :

'1787.

' MY DEAR MADAM,

' It is high time to thank you for your favour of the first of November. Indeed I have been thinking so, for two or three weeks past, and perhaps it is well for you that my engagements will not permit me to write when I please.

' Your hermitage—my imagination went to work at that, and presently built one. I will not say positively as pretty as yours, but very pretty. It stood (indeed, without a foundation) upon a southern declivity, fronting a woodland prospect, with an infant river, that is a brook, running between. Little thought was spent upon the house, but if I could describe the garden, the sequestered walks, and the beautiful colours with which the soil, the shrubs, and the thickets were painted, I think you would like the spot. But I awoke, and behold it was a dream ! My dear friend William Cowper has hardly a stronger enthusiasm for rural scenery than myself, and my favourite turn was amply indulged during the sixteen years I lived at Olney. The noises which surround me in my present situation, of carriages and carts, and London cries, form a strong contrast to the sound of falling waters, and the notes of thrushes and nightingales. But London, noisy and dirty as it is, is my post : and if not directly my choice, has a much more powerful recommendation ; it was chosen for me by the wisdom and goodness of Him, whose I trust I am, and whom it is my desire to serve. And therefore I am well satisfied with it ; and if this busy imagination (always upon the wing) would go to sleep, I would not awaken her to build me hermitages ; I want none.

' The prospect of a numerous and attentive congregation, with which I am favoured from the pulpit, exceeds all that the mountains and lakes of Westmoreland can afford ; and *their* singing, when their eyes tell me their voices come from the heart, is more melodious in my ear than the sweetest music of the woods. But were I not a servant who has neither right nor reason to wish for himself, yet has the noblest wish he is capable of forming, gratified—I say, were it not for my public services, and I were compelled to choose for myself, I would wish to live near your hermitage, that I might sometimes have the pleasure of conversing with you, and admiring your flowers and garden ; provided I could likewise, at proper seasons, hear from others that joyful sound which it is now the business, the happiness, and the honour of my life to proclaim, myself. What you are pleased to say, my dear madam, of the state of your mind, I understand perfectly well ; I praise God on your behalf, and I hope I shall earnestly pray for you. I have stood upon that ground myself. I see what you yet want to set you quite at ease, and though I cannot give it you, I trust that He who has already taught you what to desire, will, in His own best time, do everything for you, and in you, which is necessary to make you as happy as is compatible with the present state of infirmity and warfare : but He must be waited *on*, and waited *for*, to do this ; and for our encouragement it is written as in golden letters over the gate of His mercy, " Ask, and ye shall receive ; knock, and it shall be opened unto you." We are apt to wonder that when what we accounted hindrances are removed, and the things which we conceived would be great advantages are put within our power, still there is a secret something in the way which proves itself to be independent of all external changes, because it is not affected by them. The disorder we complain of is *internal*, and, in allusion to our Lord's words upon another occasion, I may say, it is not that which surrounds us, it is not anything in our outward situation (provided it be not actually unlawful), that can prevent or even retard our advances in religion ; we are defiled and impeded by that which is within. So far as our hearts are right, all places and circumstances, which His wise and good providence allots us, are nearly equal ; their hindrances will prove helps ; losses, gains—and crosses will ripen into comforts ; but till we are so far apprised of the nature of our disease, as to put ourselves into the hands of the great and only Physician, we shall find, like the woman in Luke viii. 43, that every other effort for relief will leave us as it found us.

Our first thought when we begin to be displeased with ourselves, and sensible that we have been wrong, is to attempt to reform ; to be sorry for what is amiss, and to endeavour to amend. It seems reasonable to ask, what can we do more ? but while we think we can do so much as this, we do not fully understand the design of the gospel. This gracious message from the God who knows our frame, speaks home to our case. It treats us as sinners—as those who have already broken the original law of our nature, in departing from God our creator, supreme lawgiver, and benefactor, and in having lived to ourselves instead of devoting all our time, talents, and influence to His glory. As sinners, the first things we need are pardon, reconciliation, and a principle of life and conduct entirely new. Till then we can have no more success or comfort from our endeavours, than a man who should attempt to walk while his ankle was dislocated : the bone must be reduced before he can take a single step with safety, or attempt it without increasing his pain. For these purposes we are directed to Jesus Christ, as the wounded Israelites were to look at the brazen serpent (John iii. 14, 15). When we understand what the Scripture teaches of the person, love, and offices of Christ, the necessity and final causes of His humiliation unto death, and feel our own need of such a Saviour, we then know Him to be the light, the sun of the world, and of the soul ; the source of all spiritual light, life, comfort, and influence ; having access by God to Him, and receiving out of His fulness grace for grace.

' Our perceptions of these things are for a time faint and indistinct, like the peep of dawn ; but the dawning light, though faint, is the sure harbinger of approaching day (Prov. iv. 18). The full-grown oak that overtops the wood, spreads its branches wide, and has struck its roots to a proportionable depth and extent into the soil, arises from a little acorn ; its daily growth, had it been daily watched from its appearance above ground, would have been imperceptible, yet it was always upon the increase ; it has known a variety of seasons, it has sustained many a storm, but in time it attained to maturity, and now is likely to stand for ages. The beginnings of spiritual life are small likewise in the true Christian ; *he* likewise passes through a succession of various dispensations, but he advances, though silently and slowly, yet surely ; and will stand for ever.

'At the same time it must be admitted, that the Christian life is a warfare. Much within us and much without us must be resisted. In such a world as this, and with such a nature as *ours*, there will be a call for habitual self-denial. We must learn to cease from depending upon our own supposed wisdom, power, and goodness, and from self-complacence and self-seeking—that we may rely upon Him whose wisdom and power are infinite.

'It is time to relieve you; I shall therefore only add Mrs. Newton's affectionate respects. Commending you to the care and blessing of the Almighty,

'I remain, my dear madam, with great sincerity,

'Your affectionate and obliged servant,

'JOHN NEWTON.'

The failure to which Hannah More alludes in her life at Cowslip Green led her to look more deeply into the true sources and aims of life; and to see how all strong, pure, and noble life derives power from union with God through Jesus Christ, and finds its expression in a wide love for humanity and in faithful service.

One of the first results of her endeavour to write something of more weight and influence than the lively pieces which had charmed a circle of admiring friends, was the publication of an essay on 'The Importance of the Manners of the Great to General Society.' Mixing as she did among the class of persons whose manners she censures, and including among them personal friends, she felt that she had often allowed much to pass without remark which was not only wrong in itself, but which spread downwards through the lower strata of society, and did even more mischief there than in the class where it had had its origin. The desire to enter a protest against the evils existing in the upper classes of society, and the feeling now growing within her that man cannot stand alone, but is linked by inseparable ties to all his fellow-men, were the chief motives which prompted this pamphlet.

These she expresses in a letter to her sister :

'My book is now before the public, with its sounding title, "Thoughts on the Importance of the Manners of the Great to General Society." I really was fearful lest many of those with whom I live a good deal might think that my own views and theirs were too much alike. Occasions, indeed, continually occur in which I speak honestly and pointedly ; but all one can do in a promiscuous society is not so much to start religious topics as to extract from common subjects some useful and awful truth, and to counteract the mischief of a popular sentiment by one drawn from religion ; and if I do any little good, it is in this way ; and this they will in a degree endure. I find people are ready enough to join you in reprobating vice : they are not *all* vicious, but their standard, if right, is low ; it is not the standard of the Gospels. In this little book I have not gone deep : it is but a superficial view of the subject ; it is confined to prevailing practical evils. Should this succeed, I hope by the blessing of God another time to attack more *strongly the principle.* I have not owned myself the author ; not so much because of that fear of man which "worketh a snare," as because, if anonymous, it may be ascribed to some better person ; and because I fear I do not live as I write. I hope it may be useful to myself, at least, as I give a sort of public pledge of my principles, to which I pray I may be enabled to act up.'

The book went into five editions before the end of the year. Hannah More was still in town, and wherever she went heard it discussed, and guesses made at the author. It was at first

ascribed to Wilberforce, then to the Bishop of London.
'When the author is discovered,' Hannah More writes, 'I
shall expect to find almost every door shut against me; *mais
n'importe*, I shall only be sent to my darling retirement.' But
the secret soon crept out, and by the readiness with which it
was ascribed to Hannah More, it would appear that no one
who knew her felt that the principles she expressed in the
book were incongruous with her practice; and probably she
had borne more unconscious testimony than she was aware of
to the strength of her religious principles while mixing in the
society of the day, for in writing to Mr. Newton about this
time she says, 'When I am in the great world I consider
myself as in an enemy's country, and as beset with snares,
and this puts me on my guard. Fears and snares seem
necessary to excite my circumspection; for it is certain that
my mind has more languor, and my faith less energy at
Cowslip Green, where I have no temptation from without, and
where I live in the full enjoyment and constant perusal of the
most beautiful objects of inanimate nature.' Horace Walpole
had also already bestowed upon her in good-humoured raillery
the title of St. Hannah.

The book itself, although linked by its aim to the deeper
earnestness which belongs rather to the present century than
to the last, has still the cold formality and the superficial
treatment of a subject which are characteristic of the age
which was then passing away. Outside change is nearly all
which is asked for; the deeper principles of life are not
sounded. 'The great' are the rich and titled; they are to be
the leaders of the world; the other classes simply follow them
without independent action on fixed principles. 'The great,'
on this account as much as for the sake of truth and right, are

to give up certain practices which corrupt society. These are—extravagance ; gaming ; Sabbath-breaking ; neglect of family worship ; the practice of allowing to servants the sale of the cards used in the house ; the habit of directing servants to deny admission to visitors by the social falsehood, ' *not at home ;*' Sunday concerts of sacred music ; the frequenting of public gardens on Sunday; the checking of charity by the fashionable habit of commenting constantly on the 'ingratitude of the poor,' and the calling of vices by fine names. On each of these evils Hannah More writes with good sense, and the moderation of a lady accustomed to society.

' Thoughts on the Importance of the Manners of the Great ' was but an introductory book to a work which Hannah More published two years afterwards, in which she fulfilled her hope that she ' might, by the blessing of God, attack more strongly *the principle.*' The second book she called ' An Estimate of the Religion of the Fashionable World.' This, like her former work, is grounded to some extent on the idea that religion spreads downward, descending from the upper to the middle and lower classes. But at that very period when Hannah More wrote to show that the religion of 'the great' was limited to one or two ideas, there was among the middle classes a far fuller theology, and a sufficient grasp of religious truths to resist the current of wild extravagance surging up from the later days of the French Revolution.

The wane of religion in the upper class is traced to several causes, the first of which is the prejudice, still surviving, which was created at the Restoration against Puritanism, when ' party was no longer confined to political distinctions, but became a part of morals, and was carried into religion. The more profligate of the Court party began to connect the idea of devotion with that of Republicanism, and to prove their aversion to the one, thought they could never cast too much ridicule on the other. It was not till piety was thus unfortunately brought into disrepute that persons of condition thought it made their sincerity, their abilities, or their good-breeding questionable to appear openly on the side of religion. Before this, a strict attachment to piety did not subtract from a great reputation. Men were not thought the worse lawyers, generals, legislators, or historians, for believing and even defending the religion of their country. The gallant Sir Philip Sidney, the politic and sagacious Burleigh, the all-accomplished Falkland, not only publicly owned their belief in Christianity, but wrote things of a religious nature. These instances, and many others which might be adduced, are not, it will be allowed, selected from among contemplative recluses or grave divines, but from the busy, the active, the illustrious, from public characters, from men of strong passions, beset with great temptations ; distinguished actors on the stage of life, whose respective claims to the title of fine gentlemen, brave soldiers, or able statesmen, have never been called in question.'

Amongst the other causes of the irreligion of the upper classes, Hannah More mentions the influence of French literature, Voltaire and Rousseau, and especially the want of religious education. Her remarks under this head have in them a good sense, which has often been wanting in later discussions on the same subject : ' Religion is the only thing in which we seem to look for the end without making use of the means ; and yet it would not be more surprising if we were to expect that our children should become artists and scholars without being bred to arts and languages, than it is to look for a Christian world without a Christian education.

Shall we expect then, since men can only become scholars by diligent labour, that they shall become Christians by mere chance ?   Shall we be surprised if those do not fulfil the offices of religion who are not trained to an acquaintance with them ? Religion, if taught at all, is taught rather *incidentally*, as a thing of subordinate value, than as the leading principle of human actions, the great animating spring of human conduct.'

Prominent amongst the drawbacks to religion arising from society, Hannah More places the 'habit of living in a crowd,' even though that crowd may consist of 'the best company,' persons intellectual, well-principled, or even eminently pious. ' So many books of rigid morality,' in which low motives for virtue are urged, such as prudence, self-interest, are also mentioned as aiding to lower the place of religion ; and others again, in which benevolence is set forth, as including in itself the whole root and principle of religion, apart from God or holiness.   Neither morality nor benevolence is the whole of religion. ' When there will be no distress to be relieved, no injuries to be forgiven, no evil habits to be subdued, there will be a Creator to be blessed and adored—a Redeemer to be loved and praised.'

In two years ' An Estimate of the Religion of the Fashionable World' passed through five editions, and seems to have been largely read by the class for whom it was written. Perhaps no one else but Hannah More could have written at that time a book on the subject of religion which would have been read by 'the fashionable world ;' but her intimate acquaintance with this circle, the complete *entrée* to it which her charming conversation and manners had given her, the general admiration she excited, and her known principles, fitted her in a very peculiar degree for the work. At the same time it will be easily seen that it required no little amount of courage and steadfastness to duty to write on such an unpopular subject for the very circle in which her little lively pieces had always met with so much applause. No attempt is made to smooth things over, but the whole book is characterized by perfect simplicity, independence and straightforwardness.

CHAPTER VIII.

THE DAWNING LIGHT.

UP to this time Hannah More's four sisters had continued to carry on the school in Bristol, spending the summer holidays every year at Cowslip Green. Thirty-three years had passed away since, as Miss Sally More told Dr. Johnson, they had set out to seek their fortunes, with nothing but a big empty house and a little *larning*. And now they had made sufficient money by their school to live upon, and to build for themselves a good house in Pulteney Street, Bath. Here they intended to reside during the winter, which Hannah generally spent in London, or in visiting friends, and they would still spend the summers together at her cottage at Cowslip Green. Their retirement from the school brought the sisters together once more, and formed for Hannah a home with natural obligations and ties, such as hitherto she had lived almost independently of. The sisters had been accustomed to lives of usefulness and order, duty having a much stronger claim upon them than pleasure, and in their intercourse with others they had had rather to seek the highest good of those around them, than merely to gratify and please. The influence therefore which they now brought into Hannah More's life was to detach her still more from the restless round of visiting among a crowd of persons, and to settle her to a more steadfast choice of her work in life, and to the concentration of her thoughts and energies upon it.

She still maintained a constant correspondence, however, at this time with nearly all the persons of note in the world ; and the many-sidedness of her character may be seen from the names of those who regarded her as a valued friend, and 'with whom she had genuine sympathy, but who had very little with one another. Thus among her frequent correspondents we find Horace Walpole, John Newton, Mr. Pepys, Dr. Horne, Mrs. Garrick, Mrs. Trimmer, Rev. Richard Cecil, Mrs. Montagu (Queen of the "Bas Bleu"), Bishop Porteus, Mr. Soame Jenyns, Mr. Wilberforce, and many others as diverse in character, but of less note.'

The sisters had also the pleasure of entertaining many of Hannah's friends at different times in the cottage at Cowslip Green, and, amongst others, John Newton, from whom we find the following characteristic letter, written on his return with Mrs. Newton from this visit :

September 7, 1791.

'In Helicon could I my pen dip,
I might attempt the praise of Mendip ;
Were bards a hundred I'd outstrip 'em
If equal to the theme of Shipham ;
But harder still the task, I ween,
To give its due to Cowslip Green !

'I send to you and by you my fivefold thanks to *five* ladies who will always be dear to my heart. I have no reason to think that I ever lived a single day so as to wish to live it over again. But were I obliged to retrace some one past week, and to choose which it should be, I think the week I spent at the foot of Mendip would certainly have its claim. I contracted a sort of friendship for Mendip while I was with you, and therefore you will not wonder that when I was at King's Weston it gave me some pleasure to see my new old friend peeping at me over the inferior hills. I immediately recognised him or her (which Miss Sally pleases), and was so foolish as almost to envy a hill, which, if it had eyes like me, might look at Cowslip Green from morning till night. I descended from King's Weston Hill, therefore, with some reluctance. What a prospect was I forced to give up! I thought, like Peter, "it is good to be here." But then neither he nor I was designed to spend our days on the top of a hill, however glorious the prospect. He had something better to do for his Lord, and so, I hope, have I. If so, farewell then the happy retirement of Mendip, and the view of it from King's Weston, and welcome the noise and dirt of Cheapside and of Coleman Street.'

We have now brought Hannah More's life down towards the close of the eighteenth century. We have seen her a woman of that century, living in the very centre of its intellectual life, and manifesting in herself many of its tendencies. The change we shall find henceforward in her character and in the aim and work of her life must not be ascribed merely to an individual awakening to the true sense of life and its higher purposes, nor to merely personal growth. Hannah More's course was undoubtedly one in which she constantly ' forgot those things which were behind in pressing on to those things which were before ;' but the deeper earnestness and the wider sympathy and love into which we find her passing were not peculiar to her as an individual in that age. She was, however, particularly susceptible to the best influences at work ; she allowed neither pride nor prejudice to close her mind against these, but opened her whole nature to receive the clearer light dawning on the world, and to drink in the early dew of the coming day. Thus we shall find that she not only was ready for the work of her time, but was able to give an impulse to general progress, and to sow the seeds for thought for the future.

One of the most striking features of the earlier part of the eighteenth century is its indifference to human suffering and life ; coldness and egotism everywhere prevailed ; satire fed the bitterness and cynicism of the age with scoffs at humanity ; all its deformities and weaknesses were exhibited to view, and made the subject of mocking jest ; there was no respect for man as 'the noblest work of God,' no tenderness nor pity for his fall, no regard for his inalienable rights. The result of this spirit may be seen in the slave-trade abroad ; the utter ignorance and degradation of the poor at home, in the treatment of criminals in prisons, and in the frequent executions. Even the Church of Christ itself seemed to have lost sight of the command to 'go into all the world, and preach the gospel to every creature.'

Against this narrowness that cramped the very heart of humanity there arose towards the end of the century a vigorous reaction, out of which sprang some very strong convictions of certain new ideas, or rather of certain lost truths, for they were really principles lying in the very foundation of Christianity. The feeling was gaining ground that all mankind formed but one family, that each brother had his rights, and all had claims on one another. In France this perception expressed itself in the words, soon empty enough, ' Liberty, Equality, and Fraternity.' In England, the first to recognise the truth and give it its due place were the most earnest Christians of the day, for they saw in it at once the forgotten teaching of Christ their Lord, the Divine Son of Man.

Howard visited the prisons ; Wilberforce roused England to the guilt of the slave-trade ; Raikes began to care for the little children of the poor, and to gather them into Sunday schools ; the heathen of distant lands were for the first time acknowledged to have claims upon their Christian brethren ; and Cowper, the most Christian poet of the time, raised his song in the dark gloom around him, and sang :

'How then should I and any man that lives
Be strangers to each other ?
What edge of subtlety canst thou suppose
Keen enough (wise and skilful as thou art),
To cut the link of brotherhood by which
One common Maker bound me to the kind ?
Bone of my bone, and kindred souls to me.'

One of the first expressions of Hannah More's sympathy with this rising feeling of the time is in her little poem on 'Slavery,' written, as she says, 'in such a hurry as no poem should ever be written in ; but good or bad, if it does not come out at the particular moment when the discussion comes on in Parliament, it will not be worth a straw : here time is everything.'

The poem begins with an apostrophe to Liberty, demanding why her sun, intended to shine equally on all, should only bless the north.

'Why should fell darkness half the south infest ?
Why lies sad Afric quenched in total night ?'

The equal worth and right of every man to all the blessings
life can afford are vigorously expressed, and some of the best
lines Hannah More ever wrote are in this poem. It must be
remembered that while the sentiment they express is familiar
enough to us, and beyond dispute, it required no little courage
at the time to exclaim :

> 'Perish th' illiberal thought which would debase
> The native genius of the sable race !
> Perish the proud philosophy, which sought
> To rob them of the powers of *equal thought !*
> Does then the immortal principle within
> Change with the casual colour of the skin ?
> Does matter govern spirit ? or is mind
> Degraded by the form to which 'tis joined ?
> No ; they have heads to think and hearts to feel,
> And souls to act with firm, if erring zeal ;
> For they have keen affections, kind desires,
> Love strong as death, and active patriot fires :
> All the rude energy, the fervid flame,
> Of high-souled passion and ingenuous shame ;
> Strong but luxuriant virtues boldly shoot
> From the wild vigour of the savage root.

> 'Hold, murderers, hold, nor aggravate distress,
> Respect the passions *you yourselves possess :*
> E'en you, of ruffian heart and ruthless hand,
> Love your own offspring and your native land.
> Oh, think how absence the loved scene endears
> To him whose food is groans, whose drink is tears.
> If warm your heart to British feeling true,
> As dear his land to him as yours to you ;
> And liberty, in you a hallowed flame,
> Burns unextinguished in his breast the same.
> Then leave him holy freedom's cheering smile,
> The heaven-taught fondness for the parent soil ;
> Revere affections mingled with our frame,
> In every nature, every clime the same :

> In all these feelings equal sway maintain ;
> In all the love of home and freedom reign ;
> And Tempe's vale and parched Angola's sand
> One equal fondness of their sons command.'

Then passing from the slave-dealer, with no regard for the brotherhood of men, Hannah More addresses all tyrants and oppressors, who ' make millions wretched ' for the sake of gain or power :

> ' In reason's eye, in wisdom's fair account,
> Your sum of glory boasts a like amount ;
> The means may differ, but the end's the same,
> *Conquest is pillage with a finer name.*
> Who makes the sum of human blessings less,
> Or sinks the stock of general happiness,
> Though erring fame may grace, though false renown
> His life may blazon, or his memory crown ;
> Yet the last audit shall reverse the cause,
> And God shall vindicate His broken laws.'

The poem concludes with the prayer :

> ' And Thou ! great Source of nature and of grace,
> Who of one blood didst form the human race ;
> Look down in mercy in Thy chosen time,
> With equal eye on Afric's suffering clime ;
> Disperse her shades of intellectual night,
> Repeat Thy great command, Let there be light !
> Bring each benighted soul, great God, to Thee,
> And with Thy wide salvation make them free.'

CHAPTER IX.

MENDIP.

WE have spoken of the rise and growth of the idea of the brotherhood of humanity as characteristic of the opening of the present century. As a Christian truth it had had its place in the very foundation of Christianity, but since the Reformation its recognition had been but slight, and had led to very little practical effort. This may be accounted for by the fact that the Church of the Reformation was distinctly combative ; it had to struggle through persecution and attacks of different kinds ; hence all its energies were concentrated on self-defence and the maintenance of its own existence. The religious earnestness of the Puritans was also exhausted in struggles for ecclesiastical freedom, and for purity of life amidst the active sources of corruption in the world around them. It seems strange to us now, when we endeavour to realize the fact, that the most earnestly religious man of those times did little for the ignorant and miserable around him, and nothing for the heathen nations abroad. This has led to an idea, that the source of the love which has taught us to call all men brethren, must be looked for outside of Christianity.

But whatever quarter we choose to fix upon, as the point from which the light arose to dawn upon our age, is of little moment, while this fact remains, that the followers of Christ alone have carried out the truth into practical, self-sacrificing work for others. As a beautiful sentiment the idea found a home in many hearts; and here and there one or two noble natures rose to the practice of it as a principle; but to live a true life of love, of love wide as the bounds of human existence, and tender and deep as its sorrows and needs, demands a self-denial which common natures are not in themselves capable of exercising. Only the spirit and life of Christ in men can raise communities and masses of ordinary human beings into those organizations for the help of humanity, which are the special glory of our own century; and we may add, that only Divine power working in human effort can give life and efficacy to the work, so as to make it really regenerating. If we look at any scheme or system now at work for the good of humanity in any form, we shall find that there are none in which the Church of Christ has no concern or part, either recognised or unrecognised. Thus the seeds of 'Liberty, Equality, and Fraternity,' which in France fell into barren ground, found in England the fertile soil of 'honest and good' Christian hearts, in which the Spirit of Christ dwelt; and by this Spirit the love of men passed into earnest, devoted service.

We must now see how Hannah More did not rest satisfied with singing the praise of liberty, and with proclaiming the equality and claims of all men upon all that makes this life and the life to come blessedness and joy. She gave herself to the work of serving others; and it was now no longer 'the great' who claimed her love and help—those who could repay her by admiration and applause. The poorest and most degraded, amongst whom she met with the severest trials of malignant opposition and false accusation, became the objects of her care.

We must also notice that the work to which she devoted herself was at that time new ; there was none of that literature of 'good works,' which has thrown a fame around all efforts to raise the degraded classes, and which holds out example and hope to beginners in the present day. She and her sister Patty were the pioneers in the field, breaking up new ground, and with no materials but what they had to make for themselves as they went along. It must be remembered, also, that Hannah More was not in the position of a young lady of the present day, who is tired of doing nothing, and of being nobody at home, and 'longs for a work and a sphere.' She belonged to a brilliant circle in society, in which she was courted and flattered, as few other women have been. At that very time Mrs. Siddons was acting her play of 'Percy' in London, and Horace Walpole was 'raving' at her for not coming up to town to see the great actress personate her own heroine. Whatever she wrote was read eagerly, and without criticism. Every year we find new names of rank and note added to her list of friends and correspondents.

The work to which Hannah More and her sister Patty devoted henceforth their best energies extended over a period of upwards of thirty years ; but it will be more interesting to make the sketch of it continuous, and then to return to Hannah More's literary labours and social life during this period, for at the same time it must be kept in mind that some of her best and most thoughtful productions were written during these years, and a constant correspondence and intercourse maintained with many old and new friends.

Cowslip Green was situated near the Mendip Hills, a long

limestone ridge, extending from Wells in Somersetshire to the Bristol Channel at Bream Down. According to tradition these hills had been inhabited from the earliest times by a rude race of quarrymen and miners. In the old Glastonbury legends, the holy men who founded the Christian settlement on the Isle of Avalon, where Glastonbury now stands, are said to have passed over the water, and carried the gospel to the savages of Mundean, or Mendip; yet since that time apparently no kind of light or teaching had been brought to them, and generation after generation had grown up and passed away in utter ignorance and savage lawlessness.

The attention of Hannah More was first drawn to the state of these people by Mr. Wilberforce; he had come with his sister to spend a few days at Cowslip Green, and was persuaded by Miss Patty More to pay a visit to the cliffs of Cheddar. On his return she asked him how he liked the cliffs. He replied 'that they were very fine, but the poverty and distress of the people were dreadful.' The rest of the day Mr. Wilberforce spent in his room, and the sisters feared he was unwell, but at supper he appeared, and his first words were: 'Miss Hannah More, something *must* be done for Cheddar.' He then told them of the state of the people, no spiritual teacher of any kind, no education, no settled employment, and so utterly lawless, that on Sunday, when the men were idling on the cliffs, no honest man or woman could pass that way without danger of assault. They discussed plans together till a late hour, and at last Mr. Wilberforce exclaimed: 'If *you* will be at the trouble, I will be at the expense.'

The first idea was to open a Sunday school at Cheddar,

and in order to see if this was practicable, Miss Hannah and
Miss Patty undertook a tour of discovery through Cheddar.
They were told nothing could be done without the consent of
a Mr. C., a rich farmer, who lived ten miles from the place.
After a toilsome journey across ploughed fields and bad roads,
they reached his house, 'almost starved.' They told him
what they wished to do, at which he was very much shocked,
assuring them religion was a most dangerous thing, 'especially
to agriculture ; that it had done the greatest mischief ever
since it was introduced by the monks down at Glastonbury.'
They could do but little with him, nor with one or two other
farmers, on whom they called the next day. ' They are just
as ignorant,' says Miss Hannah More of the men, 'as the
beasts that perish ; intoxicated every day before dinner, and
plunged in such vices as make me begin to think London a
virtuous place. The incumbent is a Mr. R., who has something to do at the University of Oxford, *where he resides.* The
curate lives at Wells, twelve miles off. The incumbent of a
neighbouring parish is intoxicated about six times a week,
and is often prevented from preaching by black eyes, earned
by fighting. We saw but one Bible in all the parish, and that
was used to prop a flower-pot.'

A house was found, which by removing a partition could
form a schoolhouse, and it was taken at once by Hannah
More, on a lease *for seven years.* ' There's courage for you,'
she says to Mr. Wilberforce. The whole parish was visited
by the two ladies, and promises gained by them of children
for the school. The next thing was to find a schoolmistress.
An excellent person, Mrs. Baker, was mentioned to Hannah
More, and Mrs. Baker consented to give up all, and go into
the midst of this little better than heathen village, where,

shut out from the rest of the world, she laboured faithfully amongst these poor people.

When all was ready, Hannah and Patty More went to Cheddar, and took up their abode for a week at a little ale-house, every hour being occupied in preparations for opening the school. In this village ale-house they received Mrs. Baker, 'who,' writes Hannah More, 'arrived with the true spirit of a missionary, in a little cart, with her daughter and a spinning-mistress, on one of the wettest days imaginable. Here we all assembled in the kitchen of the little public-house, and a shoulder of mutton we had the prudence to secure at Uxbridge was devoured eagerly with much appetite. The next day we collected all the parents of this vast parish—a sight truly affecting. Poor, miserable, and ignorant, not a ray of light appeared in the mind of any single one. It was a day of dreadful consideration in every view—the deplorably dark state of the people before us—the appointment we seemed to be called to. Much prayer and much faith seemed necessary. On the 25th of October we opened our school with one hundred and forty children, with exhortations, portions of Scripture, and prayer. We attended them in procession to church. The clergyman gave us a twelve minutes' discourse, upon good Tory principles, upon the laws of the land, and the divine right of kings ; but the divine right of the King of kings seemed to be a law above his comprehension.'

The Cheddar school prospered, and then the two ladies began to teach the parents of these poor children on Sunday evenings, reading to them the Bible and a sermon. Soon about sixty attended these little meetings.

Before long they discovered that even Cheddar was not

the worst of the Mendip villages. Amongst the most depraved and wretched were Shipham and Rowther Row, two mining villages at the top of Mendip ; the people savage and depraved even beyond Cheddar, brutal in their natures, and ferocious in their manners. They began by suspecting we should make our fortunes by selling their children as slaves. No constable would venture to arrest a Shipham man, lest he should be murdered and concealed in one of their pits, and never heard of more—no uncommon case. The rector of Shipham had claimed the tithes for fifty years, but had never catechized a child or preached a sermon there for forty years.

Here a school was opened, which was soon followed by schools at Landford and Banwell, Yatton and Congresbury. The next place to be taken in hand was Nailsea. 'We here made our appearance for the first time,' writes Miss Patty in her journal, 'among the glasshouse people, and entered nineteen little hovels in a row, containing in all near two hundred people. We had already encountered savages, hard-hearted farmers, little cold country gentry, a supercilious and ignorant corporation ; yet this was unlike all other things, not only different, but greatly transcending all we had imagined. We had a gentleman with us, who being rather personally fearful, left us to pursue our own devices, which we did by entering and haranguing every separate family. We obtained the promise of twenty-seven children. The colliers even are more like human beings than the people of the glasshouses.'

Soon after this the Misses More received a deputation from the parish of Blagdon, consisting of the overseer and churchwardens, begging the ladies to be so kind as to do

6

their parish a little good. On inquiry they found this parish exceeded in wickedness, if possible, any they had yet taken in hand. The execution of a woman there for taking butter from a man, who offered it, as she thought, at too high a price, had occasioned a riot in the village and alarmed these officers. 'Had the occasion been less interesting or solemn,' writes Miss Patty, 'our interview with these deputies would have been almost ridiculous. One of them, full six feet high, implored us to come, because, he said, there were some parts of the parish where *they* were afraid to go.

'There was a little hamlet belonging to it, called Charter House, on the top of Mendip, so wicked and lawless that no one ever ventured there, and thieving had been the employment handed down from father to son for the last fifty years. The poor woman under sentence of death was an inhabitant of this place, and it was here that these tender-hearted churchwardens wished to send two nervous women, because they were personally afraid to venture into the hamlet themselves.' Want of health and time prevented the Misses More from consenting immediately, 'but the crying necessities of these poor creatures prevailed.' Nothing daunted, the two sisters visited this desperate place, and in October opened there 'one of the largest, most affecting, and interesting schools we have had. One hundred and seventy young people attended, from eleven to twenty years of age, amongst them the three children of the woman about to be hanged. Several of the grown-up youths had been tried at the last assizes. Nothing we had before experienced surpassed the ignorance of these poor creatures. *Not one* out of the hundred and seventy could make any reply to the question,

Who made you? One of the men from Charter House had been tried for murder.'

Some idea may be formed of the terrible state of the country poor in England from the preceding extracts ; and it must be remembered that, unlike those in our great cities, not even crime and its dangers had in their case been turned into a means for sharpening the perceptions ; they were as dull, as sunk in intellectual degradation as in moral night. The work in our ragged schools and reformatories cannot be compared with the hopeless, heavy task of bringing the light to these rural savages. Other difficulties there were arising from the scattered nature of the work in ten different parishes, extending over a district of more than thirty miles ; the roads also were not only rough, but highly dangerous ; many a time Miss Patty records in her journal an upset at night in returning from some out-of-the-way village among the Mendip Hills, and the wild state of the country exposed them to constant danger from robbers.

One of the greatest difficulties, however, lay in the want of materials. Teachers and books for the poor were not in existence ; these they had to make for themselves, like the Israelites working without straw. 'The teaching of the teachers is not the least part of the work,' writes Hannah More to one of her friends ; 'add to this, that having about thirty masters and mistresses, with under-teachers, one has continually to bear with the faults, the ignorance, the prejudices, humours, misfortunes, and *debts* of all those poor well-meaning people. I hope, however, it teaches one forbearance, and it serves to put me in mind how much God has to bear with from *me*. I now and then comfort Patty in our journey home by night, by saying, that if we do these people no good, I hope we do some little good to ourselves.' And Hannah More certainly did not look back on such occasions to the evenings she had spent in town in the gay assemblies of 'the great,' nor in the brilliant *coteries* of the 'blue-stockings,' with any wish to find herself there, instead of rambling homewards in an old chaise in the dark over the rough roads with her sister Patty ; for further on in the same letter she writes words finer than all her wittiest and best remarks in society : ' I care little to have to do with "the great ;" I have devoted the remnant of my life to the poor, and to those that have no helper ; and if I can do them little good, I can at least sympathize with them, and I know there is comfort for a forlorn creature to be able to say, " There is somebody that cares for me." That simple idea of being *cared* for has always appeared to me a very cheering one. Besides this, the affection they have for us is a strong engine with which to lift them to the love of higher things ; and though I believe others work successfully by terror, yet kindness is the instrument with which God has enabled me to work. Alas ! I might do more and better ; pray for me that I may.'

In the work undertaken by Miss Hannah and Miss Patty More, they had no other guide than the wisdom they sought from God working together with their own good sense ; but they had firm unshaken faith, all the stronger and purer because they were imitating no one, walking in no trodden path. It is interesting now, especially to those engaged in similar work, to read of the means used by the Misses More, and to see the blessed results following them. Religion was made the very foundation of the intellectual, moral, and social change. It was the lever which elevated every part of the degraded condition of these poor human beings ; and we must notice also that it was religion in the hands of two highly educated, cultured women, with large experience of life, knowledge of the world and of human nature. They were no ignorant, unskilled workwomen, trusting alone to the magic of certain words and phrases, or to the force of one or two ideas ; they rather shunned than sought any attempt to play upon the feelings ; every part of their work aimed, through well-adapted means, at a practical result.

Hannah More's easy address and readiness in conversation, gained in society, were now brought to bear upon her work, while Patty More's school-life had no less been a most fitting training for her. Hannah More, in a letter to Mr. Bowdler, thus sketches the plans they adopted for raising and Christianizing the lowest classes : 'My plan for instructing the poor is very limited and strict. They learn of week-days such coarse works as may fit them for servants. My object has not been to teach dogmas and opinions, but to form the lower class to habits of industry and virtue. I know no way of teaching morals but by infusing principles of Christianity, nor of teaching Christianity without a thorough knowledge of Scripture. In teaching in our Sunday schools the only books we use are two little tracts called " Questions for the Mendip Schools," the Church Catechism (these are hung up in frames, half a dozen in a room), spelling-books, Psalters, Common Prayer Book, and Bible. The little ones learn " Watts's Hymns for Children." They repeat the collect every Sunday. In some of the schools a plain printed sermon and a printed prayer are read in the evening to the grown-up scholars and parents, and a psalm is sung. When we are present my sister or I read them ; in our absence the schoolmistress. The clergy-

man chooses them, and is generally present. For many years
I have given away annually near two hundred Bibles, Common Prayer Books, and Testaments. To teach the poor to
read without providing them with safe books has always
appeared to me a dangerous measure. This induced me to
the laborious undertaking of the "Cheap Repository" tracts,
which had such great success that above *two millions* were
sold in one year.

'In some parishes, where the poor are numerous, and where
there are no gentry to assist them, I have instituted Friendly
Benefit Societies for poor women, which have proved a great
relief in times of sickness, especially in the late seasons of
scarcity and distress. We have raised in the parish of Cheddar
only, a fund of nearly £300 ; in Shipham very nearly as
much. This money I have placed out in the stocks. We have
two little annual festivals for the children and poor women,
which are always attended by as many of the gentry as we can
assemble. As the morals of my own sex are the great object
of my regard, I have made it a standing rule at these anniver-
saries that every young woman brought up in my school, and
belonging to the club, who has been married during the
preceding year, and can produce a testimonial of her good
conduct from the parish minister and schoolmistress, is
presented by me with five shillings, a pair of white stockings
of our own knitting, and a handsome Bible. This trifling
encouragement has had a very good effect, for we have had to
create the regard for virtue, and sobriety and modesty are
now considered as necessary to the establishment of a young
woman.

'The grand subject of instruction with me is the Bible itself,
the familiar use of which I greatly prefer to any abridgments,

histories, or expositions. To infuse a large quantity of Scripture into their minds, with plain practical comments in the way of conversation, is the means which I have found, under God, most instrumental in forming the principles and directing the hearts of youth. God has promised His blessing on His Word. The great thing is to get it *faithfully* explained, in such a way as shall be likely to touch the heart and *influence the conduct*. I usually make them get by heart some of the most important chapters, such as the Sermon on the Mount, and many of the psalms. I delight much in familiarizing them with the histories in Genesis, as they furnish such abundant matter for practical illustration, and suggest striking applications to their own hearts and lives. To make good members of society (and this can only be done by making good Christians) has been my aim. Speculative doctrines I always avoid; but with the plain leading doctrines of Scripture they ought to be well acquainted. *Principles, and not opinions*, are what I labour to give them.'

It is almost impossible to form any accurate idea of the results of such a work as Hannah More and her sister were engaged in. If the work itself be true, much of the effects will be hidden from human sight; all labour which is brought to bear upon the soul of man must be supported by faith and confident trust that the blessing of God does make vital the good seed, and that it is as surely germinating as is the corn-seed in the dark earth of the ploughed field, before the green shoots appear. To work only for results, to look constantly for them, to exhibit them to others, and to make them alone the ground of hopefulness, is but a shallow egotism rather than a true devotion.

No account of the success which followed the labours of

Hannah More and her sister was ever published by them ; in some of Hannah More's letters to Mr. Wilberforce and Mr. Thornton, both of whom supplied money for their work, details of results are given ; and in letters to other correspondents there are allusions to encouragements in connection with their schools in the various Mendip villages. It was not until many years after both the sisters had passed away from earth that an account of their work and some of its results was published, under the name of 'Mendip Annals,' edited by Mr. Roberts, the son of Hannah More's old friend and biographer. This book is almost a reprint of a journal kept by Miss Patty More. On the cover of the book she had written, 'I have not imitated Xenophon;' for with true heroism she had entered the enemy's country, thoroughly resolved, let the result be what it might, victory or failure, she would never retreat from the field. In this journal she notes down various things she wished to keep in memory respecting the different schools. And again and again we read of sinners the most hardened and brutal brought to repentance and melting into love as they laid hold of the great truth of the gospel—help and salvation in Jesus Christ.

Two years after the Cheddar school had been begun, Miss Patty More records in her journal, 'Cheddar as usual was reserved for the great reward. Here boys and girls, old and young, men and women, all seemed blended together to sing their Maker's praises, and to cry aloud that a Redeemer is at length found in Cheddar. Here the great work evidently goes on—the people hunger and thirst—the church is filled—families pray—children are early brought to the knowledge of God—and, as a proof of their sincerity, are the means of being permitted to bring their parents. Thus shall this seemingly forgotten people, buried as it were in their own cliffs, at length become an enlightened race, praising and glorifying the Giver of all things. Our expectations during the winter had been considerable, and we found the children in general had made great progress. The young men and women appear to have increased in knowledge and grace. O Lord, do Thou enable them to press forward ! Three young men were added to their number, who discovered strong signs of repentance. One, in particular, seemed dreadfully struck with his own depravity. I never heard any creature deplore his fallen nature so affectingly. However, he has since, by Divine assistance, been shown the redemption of sinners by the death and sufferings of a Saviour, and he is more cheerful and composed.'

Then of Nailsea : 'The first letter we received confirmed the growing prosperity, not only of Cheddar, but of Nailsea. The poor colliers are daily being strengthened in their good intentions, and become hourly more serious. The room overflows at the evening reading. We can now boast (but oh ! let it be with fear and trembling, yet still with rejoicing) that we have a righteous coal-pit. The present prosperity at Nailsea calls loud for thankfulness, and the looking to such a hopeful futurity will, or should, excite a spirit of prayer. An old man in one of the poor-houses was certainly brought to a deep sense of religion by the reading of the chapter and prayers, morning and evening. Most interesting indeed was his account of himself, of his former and present state ; crying aloud that the prayers had struck conviction into his heart, and had been the saving of his soul. In short, a more humble and sincere Christian one has seldom seen. Many, no doubt, are turned from a life of sin to a life of holiness, and will praise the Lord to all eternity.

'At Uxbridge there is certainly a material improvement.

'At Shipham, the land of labour, but still of hope, we have the certainty of much improvement in the knowledge of the Scriptures, and great acquirements in reading. We wait with patience for Divine grace to operate upon the heart, and then Shipham shall shine as bright as Cheddar.

'The smaller schools of Landford and Banwell are certainly improving. We trust many are training for future holiness.

'Yatton gives us some comfort, and Congresbury can *read* the Bible.

'Thus are nearly a thousand children in training, at all events, for the mansions of the blessed, and thus in *ten* villages will the Saviour's name be known at last. So ends '93. May we consider ourselves not only the Lord's *willing*, but His *waiting* servants, that nothing may ever discourage us.'

This report relates, it must be remembered, to only two years' labour in the oldest school, Cheddar; the others were all of a later date. As the work spread beneath the surface, and the children in the schools grew up, the change in the whole condition of the population of this part of the country became most marked. The habits of the people were altered ; 'old things were passing away, and all things seem to be made new.' Again and again the county justices find the number of criminals brought before them diminishing year by year. Even at Blagdon, in that village on the top of Mendip into which no officer dared to enter, the justice desires that the 'Miss Mores may be publicly informed of the extraordinary decorum of the men on the day of their club, their conduct having struck all parties. We ventured to infer from this,' adds Miss Patty, 'that religion was evidently operating upon their conduct, and were much rejoiced.'

Of the means which God thus abundantly honoured and blessed we notice two features. First, the honour which was given in all the teaching of Patty and Hannah More to the moral law of God. It was 'the schoolmaster' to bring these degraded human beings to Christ. For they were distinctly shown at once what was its high standard, that they might see how they had fallen from it ; and the hope held forth to them in Jesus Christ was the hope of power and life to rise from the slavery of sin to the obedience of God's law. Salvation from sin was to be a return to God.

Secondly, the means employed were neither new nor singular. It consisted in a wide and intelligent teaching of the Word of God, not of single verses picked out of it as mere motives ; but the whole Bible was read, and considerable portions of it learned by heart. Old Testament narratives, the Psalms, the Gospels and Epistles—all were used as necessary to a well-founded piety, and a steadfast, righteous life.

CHAPTER X.

THE 'CHEAP REPOSITORY' TRACTS.

THE work of Hannah More and her sisters in the Mendip villages soon brought strongly before them the fact that, while in all their schools they were teaching children to read, there was little or no literature of a wholesome character and popular style which could find its way into the hands of the lower classes. It is difficult now to realize the state of things with which these earnest women had to contend, or to imagine what our work among the poor would be were every tract, magazine, and popular story suppressed. The literature of the time was written for educated readers of a certain class, and in language so far removed from our daily homely English, that the words would be as strange to an ignorant person as a foreign language; while the expense of books alone shut them up from the poor. The only reading which they could procure was the ballads and sheets sold by the hawkers, and these were for the most part of a foul and degrading character. Beyond these there were a few pamphlets, which had been written in the early days of the French Revolution, by persons anxious to spread French infidelity in England, and to stir up the working classes to lawless revolt.

To supply the terrible want of sound and helpful literature

for those to whom they had given the power over the world
of thought and imagination which comes with the ability to
read, Hannah More and her sister Sally determined to set to
work to write lively stories, ballads, and songs, such as should
treat of the common life of the poor, with its trials and temptations ; and which should set before them the best ideals
they could draw of persons under the same circumstances,
who bravely did their best and overcame through the might
of faith, industry, and self-denial. They had no models of
successful works of this kind upon which to form their own.
They had to adopt a style with which no doubt they were now
familiar in their intercourse with the poor, but which they
had never used themselves through the many years of their
past life. They had also to get their writings printed in a
cheap form, so as to sell them at a price hitherto unheard of
in the annals of publishing. Hannah More's plan was to
produce every month three tracts, consisting of stories or
ballads, written in the language of the people, and which
should be sold to the hawkers at a lower rate than their usual
books and songs, so that for the sake of the better profit they
might have every inducement to sell these in preference.

During the first year the plan was so far successful that two
millions of the ' Cheap Repository ' Tracts, as they were called,
were sold. Many of these found their way into the hands of
Hannah More's very large circle of friends and acquaintances ;
but allowing for a few thousand remaining in the possession
of those persons who were curious to see what the late *bas-
bleu* could have to say to the poor, a very large proportion
were carried into the homes of the class for which they were
intended. In this work Hannah More had the occasional
assistance of her sister Sally, whose bright intelligence and

sense of humour produced one or two of the most popular of
the tracts ; she also obtained the help of two or three friends ;
but so great was the gulf which then existed between the
upper and lower classes, that very few persons had the least
idea of how to write for any class but their own. Most of the
work had, therefore, to be done by Hannah More herself. To
this she applied herself for three years, bringing out three new
tracts every month, and setting aside for this all other literary
work. It is needless to say that the toil, as regards money,
was wholly unremunerative. The plan, on the other hand,
could not be carried out without considerable expense ; and
the time it demanded prevented her from carrying on her
other writings, by which she always made a large sum of
money every year.

Hannah More has the honour of being the first writer who
addressed herself directly to the poor, and who endeavoured
to make literature a means of bringing light and help into
lives sunk in sordid toil, or the deeper degradation of mere
brutal existence. She has had many followers, who in the
wider sympathy of the present day have known better how to
reach the human hearts of their brothers and sisters struggling
with the difficulties of earning their bread by labour. But to
take the first step in a new course demands always more
courage and resolution, more faith and steadfastness to duty,
than to follow where others lead the way. Hannah More's
name must, therefore, always be held in the esteem due to all
brave pioneers in a march over untrodden ground.

Her work in this good cause is characterized by her relation
to the eighteenth and nineteenth centuries. She shows in it
the full recognition of the right of every class in the community
to the light and development enjoyed hitherto by the few ;

and she sets herself with earnest purpose to help to raise
those below, catching the spirit of the coming age, and fore-
stalling its work. But the tone of the tracts, the assertion of
superiority, the style of writing, and the tendency to deal only
with the outside life and habits of the poor, belong to the
period in which she had first begun to take rank herself in
the literary world. As in her other writings, so in these for
the poor, the principles on which they are grounded are those
of common sense and obedience to all the laws of God. It is
to a life spent in strict accordance with these that she
points as the ideal life in which happiness and comfort are to
be found.

One of the best specimens of Hannah More's 'Cheap
Repository' Tracts is the 'History of Tom White.' He
begins life as the son of an honest labourer in Wiltshire. As
soon as he is big enough he goes into service at Farmer
Hodges' as waggon-boy. The farmer makes him read the
Bible every evening, and 'would have turned him out of his
service if he had ever gone into the ale-house for his own pleasure.' Tom has to go with the waggon to the Bear Inn, at
Devizes, then on the great highway to the west, and here he
sees smart postboys, whose red jackets and tight boots make
him ashamed of his carter's smock. He resolves to be a postboy, 'drive a chaise and see the world.' By degrees Tom
falls by the temptations of his new life. He learns to swear,
to drink ' for the sake of being thought merry company and a
hearty fellow.' He leaves off going to church, and 'does not
know a Sunday at last from a Monday.' He gets money,
but ' fives, cards, cudgel-playing, and laying wagers ' soon run
away with it.

At last, in driving a race with another postboy through

Brentford, his chaise is upset, and with his leg broken in two places, Tom finds himself in a London hospital. His life hitherto had been in violation of God's laws, and trouble and sorrow are shown to be the result of such a course. In the hospital Tom sees this himself; he heartily repents; sends for his Bible and Prayer Book; resolves by God's help to lead a different life in the future. On his discharge he doubts whether he ought to return to his old employment as postboy; but Hannah More never represents those things as sinful which are not real and actual breaches of God's commands; Tom is made, therefore, to reply to his thoughts thus: 'But,' says he, sensibly enough, 'gentlefolks must travel; travellers must have chaises, and chaises must have drivers; 'tis a very honest calling, and I don't know that goodness belongs to one sort of business more than another; and he who can be good in a state of great temptation, provided the calling be lawful, and he be diligent in prayer, may be better than another man, for aught I know; and all that belongs to us is to do our duty in that state of life in which it shall please God to call us.'

Tom becomes again a postboy, but strives now at all times to order his life by the laws of God. He becomes thus careful, civil, neat, and industrious; is good to his horses, 'because he has read in the Bible that "a good man is merciful to his beast."' He is a favourite on the road, gets well paid, and 'being frugal, he spent little; and having no vices, he wasted none. He soon found out that there was some meaning in the text which says that "godliness hath the promise of the life that now is, as well as of that which is to come."' By the advice of Farmer Hodges, Tom at last takes a small farm, and here the 'regularity, sobriety, peaceableness, and piety of his daily life,' make him a pattern to the parish. But Farmer White soon finds that his house wants a mistress ; acting on the Bible assertion, that he that findeth a good wife receives her from God, he 'prays to God to direct him in so important a business.' He soon hears of a young woman who lived as upper maid in the vicar's family. 'She was prudent, sober, industrious, and religious. Her neat, modest appearance at church was an example to all persons in her station. It was her character, however, which recommended her to Farmer White. He knew that "favour is deceitful, and beauty is vain ; but a woman that feareth the Lord, she shall be praised." "Ay, and *not only praised, but chosen too,*" says Farmer White, as he took down his hat from the nail, in order to go and wait on the vicar and ask his consent.'

They are married ; and on the wedding-day, after advice from the vicar, Tom White concludes, 'I could tell you, sir, not as a thing that I have read in a book, but as a truth I feel in my own heart, that to fear God and keep His commandments will not only bring a man peace at last, but will surely make him happy now, for the commands of God are the best laws for this world.'

As a good specimen of the ballads written by Hannah More for the people we may take 'Turn the Carpet ; or, the Two Weavers :'—

> 'As at their work two weavers sat,
> Beguiling time with friendly chat,
> They touched upon the price of meat,
> So high, a weaver scarce could eat.
>
> "What with my brats and sickly wife,"
> Quoth Dick, "I'm almost tired of life ;
> So hard my work, so poor my fare,
> 'Tis more than mortal man can bear.

"How glorious is the rich man's state !
His house so fine ! his wealth so great !
Heaven is unjust, you must agree.
Why all to him?   Why none to me?

"In spite of what the Scripture teaches,
In spite of all the parson preaches,
This world (indeed, I've thought so long)
Is ruled, methinks, extremely wrong.

"Where'er I look, where'er I range,
'Tis all confused, and hard, and strange ;
The good are troubled and oppressed,
And all the wicked are the blessed."

Quoth John, "Our ignorance is the cause
Why thus we blame our Maker's laws ;
Parts of His ways alone we know,
'Tis all that man can see below.

"Seest thou this carpet, not half done,
Which thou, dear Dick, hast well begun?
Behold the wild confusion there,
So rude the mass, it makes one stare.

"A stranger ignorant of the trade
Would say no meaning's there conveyed :
For where's the middle, where's the border?
Thy carpet, sure, is all disorder."

Quoth Dick, "My work is yet in bits,
But still in every part it fits ;
Besides, you reason like a flout—
Why, man, that carpet's inside out."

Says John, "Thou say'st the thing I mean,
And now I hope to cure thy spleen ;
This world, which clouds thy soul with doubt,
Is but a carpet inside out.

"As when we view these shreds and ends
We know not what the whole intends,
So where on earth things look but odd,
They're working still some scheme of God.

"No plan, no pattern can we trace,
All wants proportion, truth, and grace ;
The motley mixture we deride,
Nor see the beauteous upper side.

"But when we reach that world of light,
And view those works of God aright,
Then shall we see the whole design,
And own the workman is Divine.

"What now seem random strokes will there
All order and design appear ;
Then shall we praise what here we spurned,
For then the carpet shall be turned."

"Thou'rt right," quoth Dick, "no more I'll grumble
That this sad world's so strange a jumble ;
My impious doubts are put to flight,
For my own carpet sets me right."'

Encouraged as Hannah More was by the success of her undertaking, she was unable to keep it up for more than three years ; for very soon the whole labour of writing the tracts devolved entirely upon her, and this, in addition to her Mendip work, seriously affected her health. Fresh editions of the tracts continued, however, to be called for, and for some years they formed the larger portion of the popular literature distributed by visitors of the poor. 'The Shepherd of Salisbury Plain' is still issued by the Religious Tract Society.

CHAPTER XI.

THOROUGHLY engaged now in the earnest work of life, living for others and for God, Hannah More became more and more detached from the general society in which she had spent so much of her time during her earlier years. She now lived only two months of the year in London ; and this time was divided between her old friend Mrs. Garrick, Bishop Porteus, Lord Teignmouth, Mr. Thornton, and Mr. Hoare ; while she also met at some of these houses a circle of earnest Christians, whose spiritual life was deep and strong, and whose outward lives were manifestations of devoted love to Christ as the Saviour and Redeemer. From the tone of her tracts it might be supposed that she aimed only at an outward and moral reformation in the poor ; but the work was altogether so new that she had not yet learned to trust to the living power of the representation to the poor and ignorant of Christ's work and death for man in bringing him to God, as the principle and strength of obedience. Hannah More's own diary, kept at this time, shows, however, how completely her own heart was 'at the secret source of every precious thing.'

'*Sunday*, *January* 19, 1794.—Heard of the death of Mr. Gibbon the historian, the calumniator of the despised Nazarene, the derider of

Christianity. Awful dispensation ! He, too, was my acquaintance. Lord, I bless Thee, considering how much infidel acquaintance I have had, that my soul never came into their secret ! How many souls have his writings polluted ! Lord, preserve others from their contagion !

'*Sunday, February* 9.—This has been a hurrying week to me, in trying to raise money for the militia shoes : so much writing and talking, that there has been little leisure for reading—little disposition for communion with God. When shall I gain more self-possession ? when shall I be able to do business with the world, without catching the spirit of the world ? Another friend dead, Richard Burke ! witty, eloquent ! but how vain those talents without the one thing needful ! I thank God that He has shown me the vanity of genius, and given me a comparative deadness to reputation. Lord ! do Thou increase it, till I become quite mortified to the world. A fresh subject for praise this night—my dear friend Wilberforce carried one clause of the Slave Bill. Lord ! hasten the time when true liberty, light and knowledge shall be diffused over the whole earth.

'*March* 12.—Dined with friends at Mrs. ——. What doest thou here, Elijah ? Felt too much pleased at the pleasure expressed by so many accomplished friends on seeing me again. Keep me from contagion !

'*Sunday, March* 23.—Had a comfortable religious day. I see the need of doing the duty of every day in its day ; by not noting down the texts, I have forgotten them. When I look back on the past week, I see cause for mourning over my vanity and folly. Escaped from hurry, vexation, gaiety, and temptation, to peace, leisure, and retirement. Where I had planned much progress to my own mind—I find a languor, a drowsiness, and deadness—sloth and self-love getting strong dominion, and much time wasted which I had devoted to improvement. Let these continual discoveries make me humble. All has been peace and quiet without, and that has induced carelessness within—the calm of prosperity is not good for the soul.

'*Sunday, April* 20.—Passed this week in hurry—neither read nor prayed with fervour.

'*Sunday, May* 4.—Heard Mr. Cecil—on " the Good Shepherd, who layeth down His life for the sheep." Oh, blessed Shepherd ! receive me, Thy erring and straying sheep, into Thy fold !

'*May* 6.—Came to Fulham to my dear Bishop—much kindness—literary and elegant society ; but the habits of polished life, even of virtuous and pious people, are too relaxing. Much serious reading, but not a serious spirit; good health, with increased relaxation of mind; thus are the blessings of God turned against Himself.

'*Sunday, July* 13.—Went to Shipham and Cheddar—very full schools at each : had much comfort in the improvement of most, and the growing piety of many. We were both enabled to speak and instruct with spirit, and seemed to make an impression. Read a sermon to the aged. Came home very late and much tired, but I hope full of gratitude.

'*July* 15.—Prayed with some comfort ; but my mind was too much in other concerns. Have much business on my hands at this time ; and though it is all of a charitable and religious nature (for I humbly design never to have any other), yet still the details of it draw away my soul and thoughts from God. When shall I be purified ?

'*Wednesday, July* 23.—Gave our annual feast on Mendip to our poor children, near one thousand. Conjured by the Bishop to answer Paine's atheistical book, with a solemnity which made me grieve to refuse. Lord ! do Thou send abler defenders of Thy holy cause ! Heard of the death of Mr. W——, an awful death ! Profane, worldly, unawakened, in the extremest old age !

'*Sunday, August* 10.—Talked earnestly to sweet Mrs. F—— ; gave her Witherspoon. Have read and conversed for many days with her and Lady W——. Lord ! enable me with equal prudence and zeal to labour to impress Thy great doctrines on her heart, and at the same time let me in all humility copy her resignation. Heard of the death of young Burke. Lord ! bless this heavy loss to his broken-hearted father. Oh ! do Thou now show him the vanity of ambition, and the worthlessness of the noblest talents, except as they are used to promote Thy glory. Lord Chancellor Bathurst is gone, one of my oldest, kindest friends : I had very many obligations to him. How warnings multiply ! this week I have not made the most of my time ; vain thoughts and old besetting sins begin to resume their power. Lord ! enable me to pray more, to struggle more, to live in closer communion with Thee. Went to Sandford, Banwell school, and Church Shipham school. Patty read Walker on "If any man be in Christ, he is a new creature." A large and attentive audience. She laboured diligently ; expounded Scripture at four schools. She greatly eclipses me. Lord ! be Thou her exceeding great reward. Another month has now ended ; before it closed, I heard of the death of ten old friends ; *all* taken—*I* left. Will nothing quicken my diligence ?

'*September.*—Confined this week with four days' headache : an unprofitable time—thoughts wandering—little communion with God. I see by every fresh trial that the time of sickness is seldom the season for religious improvement. This great work should be done in health, or it will seldom be well done. Oh for better preparation for sickness and death !

'*Sunday, September* 14.—Cheddar—a very blessed day ; between three and four hundred young and old ; many seriously impressed. This has revived my hopes that God will enable us to carry on this very extensive work, notwithstanding the heavy loss of our dear schoolmistress. May we be deeply humbled under a sense of our own unworthiness for this work ! May Thy glory, and the good of souls, be our only end. *We are* nothing, *have* nothing, and of ourselves can *do* nothing.

'*Sunday, September* 21.—Stayed at home on account of the weather. Read and prayed with some degree of comfort, which was invaded by the reflection that we might have been doing good at the schools. For some days have found more comfort in prayer, more warmth in spirit ; but still lamentably defective—above all in *family prayer*. What is read by others makes little impression on me—not so in extemporary prayer. Yet I have a fear that it is novelty, or curiosity, that catches me. Lord, let my heart and not my ear be seized upon !

'*Sunday, September* 28.—Nailsea church and Yatton—had a painful, trying day. Much enmity against religious schemes ; opposition, labour, and bodily fatigue ! Yet what is this to what the Apostles and their blessed Master endured ! Lord, strengthen my faith, enable me to have patience with these ignorant opposers of Thy law. Encouraged by seeing many of our young men seriously affected ; unwilling on that account to throw up this one school, which I think we should have done, had our motives been merely human.

'When will my heart be a fit tabernacle for the Spirit of purity? Have lately had much communion with God in the night. I grow, I hope, more disposed to convert silence and solitude into seasons of prayer. I think also I fear death less. I am much tried by the temper of others. Lord, subdue my *own* evil tempers. Let me constantly think of Him 'who endured such contradiction of sinners against Himself.'

'*Sunday, October* 19.—Being hindered by heavy rains from visiting our schools, I resolve by Thy grace to devote myself this day, O Lord, in an especial manner to Thy service. I have seldom a Sabbath to spend on myself. Let me not trifle away this precious opportunity, but pass it in extraordinary prayer, reading and meditation. Enable me to make conversation one of my pious exercises.

'I desire to remember with particular gratitude in my devotions, that on this day five years, my colleague and myself set up our first religious in-stitution at Cheddar. Bless the Lord, O my soul, for the seed which was that day sown ! Do Thou daily turn more hearts from darkness to light, and preserve them from falling back again. O Lord, I desire to bless Thy holy name for so many means of doing good, and that when I visit the poor, I am enabled to mitigate some of their miseries. I bless Thee that Thou hast called me to this employment, which, in addition to many other advantages, contributes to keep my heart tender.

'*Sunday, November* 9.—I have lately been negligent in self-examination. I resolve by Thy grace to be more diligent. My faithful colleague has gone to our schools. I wish to acknowledge her superiority to myself in many principal parts of our joint concern, particularly in familiarizing Scripture to untutored minds.

'*Sunday, November,* 16.—A fatiguing day—visited five schools ; many difficulties surrounded me. Lord, increase our faith ; let the discoveries of faith be more clear, the desires of faith more strong, the dependencies of faith more firm and fixed, the dedications of faith more ardent and resolute, and the delights of faith more elevating and durable.

'*Sunday, November* 23.—Detained at home by a severe cough and head-ache. Grieved to find that when I have this last complaint to a great degree, I have seldom any strong religious feelings. I would have hoped it is because its acuteness almost destroys the power of thinking, did I not feel, to my great sorrow, that my mind rambles through a thousand vain, trifling, and worldly thoughts, even sometimes in extremity of pain ; but seldom sticks close to God and holy things. It seems a just punishment for my sinfulness, in having suffered my thoughts to roam too much in easier and happier hours, that I am deprived of the consolations of pious reflections in those moments of keen suffering, when nothing else can support the soul under the pains of the body. Lord, enable me to keep closer to Thee at other times, and then I humbly trust Thou wilt not desert me at these trying times. Enable me to fix my thoughts more intensely, more frequently, on death and dying scenes.'

'*December* 15.—Went to Bath. I have now entered a new scene of life. O Lord ! fit me for the duties and keep me from all the temptations of it. I thank Thee that the vain and unprofitable company with which this place abounds, is a burden to me. Give me a holy discretion on the one hand, and zeal not to be drawn off from better practices on the other. As my conversation will be less useful, let me be careful that my thoughts are more holy, and that I look more after the state of my heart. Give me a submissive spirit to bear all the wounding words I may be obliged to hear against religion. And do Thou remove those prejudices which obstruct the growth of some of my friends in Divine things.'

Three years later she writes :

'*January* 1, 1798.—Having obtained help of God, I continue to this day. Lord, I am spared, while others are cut off. Let me now dedicate myself to Thee with a more entire surrender than I have ever yet made.

'First. I resolve by the grace of God to be more watchful over my temper. 2ndly. Not to speak rashly or harshly. 3rdly. To watch over my thoughts : not to indulge in vain, idle, resentful, impatient, worldly imaginations. 4thly. To strive after closer communion with God. 5thly. To let no hour pass without lifting up my heart to Him through Christ. 6thly. Not to let a day pass without some thought of death. 7thly. To ask myself every night when I lie down, am I fit to die ? 8thly. To labour to do and to suffer the whole will of God. 9thly. To cure my over-anxiety, by casting myself on God in Christ.

'*Sunday, January* 7.—I will *confess* my sins. *Repent* of them. Plead the atonement. Resolve to love God and Christ. Implore the aid of the Spirit for light, strength, and direction. Examine if these things are done. Be humbled for my failures. Watch and pray.

'Through death the Christian's soul goes to—1st. Perfect purity. 2ndly. Fulness of joy. 3rdly. Everlasting freedom. 4thly. Perfect rest. 5thly. Health and fruition. 6thly. Complete security. 7thly. Substantial and eternal good.

'*Sunday, January* 21.—Up late last night—much harassed all the week by worldly company. My temper hurt—heart secularized. I had looked forward to a peaceful Sunday—instead of this, an acute headache. Spent the day in bed—little devotion—no spirituality. Could not even *think* at all. Had an hour's talk with Mr. Wilberforce—had reason to bless God that in my present difficulties this wise Christian friend was at hand to counsel and comfort me. Lord, grant that my many religious advantages may never appear against me. Many temptations this week to vanity. My picture asked for two publications. Dedications—flattery without end. God be praised, I *was not* flattered but vexed. Twenty-four hours' headache makes one see the vanity of all this ! Am I tempted to vanity ? Let me call to mind what shining friends I have lost this year—each eminent in his different way, yet he that is least in the kingdom of grace is greater than they.

'I resolved at the beginning of the year, to pray at least twice a week, separately for the country, in this time of danger, independently of the petitions offered up in my other prayers.

'*Sunday, January* 28.—I indulge too much in the thought, how much better I might be, had I fewer interruptions, more opportunity of vital preachers, more pious friends, less worldly company. There is great self-deceit in all this. Am I praying against these disadvantages? Do I make the most of the rest of my time? Lord, assist me to do so, and to bear patiently what I dislike. This week I have watched my words more, but not sufficiently my thoughts. . . . Heard of John Wilkes's death—awful event! talents how abused! Lord, who hath made *me* to differ? but for Thy grace, I might have blasphemed Thee like him. In early youth I read Hume, Voltaire, Rousseau, etc. I am a monument of mercy, not to have made shipwreck of my faith.

'*February* 2.—My birthday. Lord, grant I may never have cause to say, "it were good for me had I never been born." Lord, forgive the sins of my youth—they have pressed on me this day. Blot them from Thy book, and give me grace to subdue my remaining corruptions. Oh, how strong!

'. . . Preparing for London. Oh! that I were as anxious to forget nothing relating to the next world, as I am to omit nothing I shall want in this journey.

'Heard —— preach : elegant language, earnest and bold, but nothing to the heart ; no food for perishing sinners. Lord, send more labourers into Thy vineyard! Increase the number of those who preach Christ Jesus, and salvation through Him only.

'*Sunday, February* 25.—Came last night to Fulham Palace. Lord, while I admire these Christian friends, let me not overrate any child of man. Christ is *all.* Oh for a fuller persuasion of this!

'*Teston, March* 1.—Arrived here on Monday—seriously ill all the way. How many suffer painful journeys, who find no rest for the sole of the foot at night ; but I rest with kind Christian friends, and find every comfort and alleviation. Several bad nights—violent cough—not comforted by religious, but tormented by worldly thoughts. Oh for a sanctified suffering! Merciful Father, withdraw not Thy heavy hand until Thy work of sanctification is done in my soul.

'. . . While attending on the dying-bed of Mrs. —— I did not feel my heart properly affected. Oh that I may lay to heart this lesson of mortality! Lord, prepare me for this state of pain, weakness, imbecility, if it be Thy will I should pass through it. She is dead. I too must die.

Oh that I could learn to die daily ! and then I should look without fear to the dark valley which lies before me.

'*March* 25.—Tempted to be warm in politics. Under the mask of religion, I fear I indulge my own humours and resentments. I would learn of Him who was meek and lowly. I cannot fix my thoughts intently on death, according to my resolution. Death advances, but I do not advance in my preparation for it.

'*Monday, April* 2.—My attention has not wandered so much as usual, but my heart has not been deeply touched. I am about to leave this place. Lord, forgive what I have neglected to do, and what I have done ; and if any little good has been done by me, be pleased graciously to accept it, and forgive its imperfections. Mrs. B—— gave me largely for the poor. Lord bless her, and make all her bed in her sickness ! Strengthen her faith. Remove the prejudices that impede her comforts. Support her through life. Be her support in death, and if we never meet again here, grant that we may meet in the kingdom of our Lord Jesus Christ.

'*London, Sunday, April* 15.—I have been a week here—hurried, worldly, with little serious reading, less serious thoughts, except when I lie awake in the night : this is often a comfortable time with me—the world shut out—my conscience more tender—my memory more quick in bringing my sins before me. My temper is sore tried. Yesterday I was tempted to anger—to-day I bore the provocation. Teach me to subdue all anger, Lord, and not to think I am helping Thy cause when I am angry. Oh that I could learn of Him who was meek and lowly ! Had a little serious talk with the Duchess of Gloucester, Lady Amherst, and the Duchess of Beaufort. Lord, let me be no mean respecter of persons, but make me valiant for Thy truth.

'*Sunday, April* 29.—Had a bad headache all day—nothing done for God —in pain my religion vacillates ; I trust I am tolerably patient and resigned, yet not as becomes a disciple of the suffering Jesus. This week has been nearly passed in visiting—little reading or seriousness. A few occasions, indeed, were snatched to talk seriously to young Christians, and I bore my testimony pretty strongly in company with some learned sceptics. At another time too much carried away with the pleasure of talking on mere subjects of taste—have taken too much pains to shine, and felt too much pleasure to hear my taste commended on the subject of French literature. Spent three days at Mitcham—felt the joy of pious society. I fear I do not profit enough when I get with pious people—it evaporates in self-satisfied feelings and serious talk, without reaching the heart.

' I feel full of schemes of charity—of doing good—of promoting God's glory—of writing for usefulness, not fame : yet I can take little comfort in these evidences, because I do not feel the love of Christ constraining me.

' *Sunday, May* 20.—My journal stopped a fortnight :—busy in getting forward my " Strictures on Education." This week has been too much spent in receiving visits from the great. Lord, preserve me from these temptations to vanity. Oh, let me feel more and more that I am a miserable sinner.

' *May* 21.—A present of Lord Orford's work—my picture in the book— I laboured to hinder it. Lord, keep me from self-sufficiency, and humble me under a deep sense of the emptiness of earthly honours. He had all *this* world could give—great, witty, brilliant. Of how little importance are these things now ! " Blessed are the pure in heart, for they shall see God." Grant me this purity, and an utter indifference to fame, and deadness to the world.

' *June* 4.—Much painful feeling at Pitt's duel. Lord, show these *wise* men the Gospel, that in Thy light they may see light, for without that the wisest sit in darkness.

' *Sunday, June* 10.—Went to Nailsea. Lord, fill my heart with gratitude for the blessings of this day. Found all flourishing. One hundred and forty children. Taught the Scriptures to three poor young colliers.

' Many strangers came to see me this week. I bless God this raised in me no vanity ; nor did a flattering history of me in a public print : I desire " *that* honour which cometh from God only."

' *Sunday, August* 26.—By the mercy of God I am permitted to write once more. Lord, grant that my life, thus graciously spared, may be spent more vigorously to Thy glory. On the 13th, after two days' severe headache, fell down in a violent fit—dashed my face against the wall, and lay long seemingly dead—much bruised and disfigured ; have lain by above a fortnight almost useless ; violent pains in my head, loss of sleep. Grant, Lord, that as my outward man decays, I may be renewed in the spirit of my mind. I have lost all this time from my book, and have redeemed too little of it by serious thought. Oh for that happy state, where is neither sorrow nor crying !

' A fresh proof of human depravity has, I hope, brought me nearer to God. I have been driven nearer to Him, and have had more comfort in prayer ; but still I am not enough renewed in the spirit of my mind. Lord, perfect what is lacking in my faith and love, and let me " possess my soul in patience." Refine my zeal, purify my motives, lead me to act with a holy simplicity, leaving the event to Thee who doest all things well. Oh for purer, holier converse ; more disentanglement from the world ; more heavenly meditation !

'*Saturday, September* 22.—Head seldom free from pain. Suffering does not yet purify my heart, though my gracious Father purposes it for that end. Lord, sanctify pain to me : make me as willing to *suffer* Thy will as to *do* it. Company *every* day, *all* day ; chiefly good people, but so much company unspiritualizes my mind, and swallows up time. Book goes on slowly. Cheap Repository is closed. " Bless the Lord, O my soul !" that I have been spared to accomplish that work ! Do Thou, O Lord, bless and prosper it to the good of many ; and if it do good, may I give to Thee the glory, and take to myself the shame of its defects. I have devoted three years to this work. Two millions of these tracts disposed of during the first year ! God works by weak instruments to show that the glory is all His own.

'*Sunday, September* 30.—Have had more communion with God lately, especially in the night-watches. Thoughts more called off from worldly things, and less vexed by disappointments ; still I find it hard to fix my mind on God and eternity by day. I had rather *work* for God than *meditate* on Him ; yet Divine communion is the work of heaven, and how shall I be prepared but by this ?

'*Sunday, November* 18.—Returned from Bath in an improved state of health, as I thought ; but health being doubtless not good for me, had a return of my headache. I might turn the time lost from more active duties to good account by secret communion with my God and Saviour, but, alas ! this is too little the case—partly, indeed, that the intense pain in my head deprives me of the free exercise of thought, and gives an involuntary gloom and depression to my spirits, but more, I fear, from a habit of not sufficiently watching over my thoughts at other times. It is a grievous truth that I am in general least religious when I am sick. Lord, do Thou give me grace to improve these seasons !

'*December* 2.—Vain thoughts discompose my own mind, and evil tempers show me the emptiness of that flattery with which I am at times overwhelmed. Lord, I hope I can say that I derive little pleasure from such praises, while my heart tells me how little I deserve them. I compare myself with the purity of Thy law, and then I see my own sinfulness too plainly to be pleased by flattering words. Heard of a silly and humiliating history of myself just published, and can truly say it gave me little or no mortification ; nor did I feel any desire to contradict it.

'*Sunday, December* 23.—Ill above a week with violent cough—blistered, etc. By the grace of God I am resigned to pain, but my thoughts, which ought at such times to be devoted to heavenly things, are not always in my own power—they wander amidst the vanities and cares of earth, instead of being directed straight forward to the goal to which I am tend- ing. Lord, raise my grovelling affections to Thyself—disperse these earthly vapours which obscure my faith—increase my desires after that world where sin and sorrow will be done away !

'An awful dispensation ! the curate of —— visited with sudden blindness for three days—it seems to have been a supernatural awakening. Lord, do Thou perfect this work : do Thou call this man out of darkness to Thy marvellous light, for his own sake, and the sake of those many souls over whom he is set !

'Heard of the dangerous illness of Mr. Cecil. Lord, I bless Thee that Thou hast enabled this faithful servant to bear his agonies as a Christian, and that his sufferings have not slackened his faith. Raise him up, if it be Thy will, for further usefulness ; but if not, sustain him in his last conflict, and enable him to bear his dying testimony to Thy faithfulness and truth ; and do Thou supply his place so that his people shall not miss his services.

'*December* 31.—I am now, by the great mercy of God, brought to the end of another year. Lord, enable me to consider this mercy as I ought to do, and do Thou strengthen my memory to recollect the numberless favours I have received at Thy hands during the course of it. Enable me to call to mind my trials, and to lament my sins of the past year. Lord, forgive whatever fresh guilt I have contracted. O wash me clean in the blood of the everlasting covenant ; forgive whatever I have done amiss, whatever I have neglected to do. Supply all my wants out of Thine abundant mercies. Strengthen my weakness, subdue my pride, heal my self-love, root out my evil tempers, deliver me from open anger, secret resentments, and discontents ; deliver me from myself, from the corruptions of my own evil heart, from the suggestions of unbelief ; and do Thou sanctify to me the mercies and deliverances of the past year. Thou hast preserved my colleague and myself from many dangers. Thou hast pre- served our going out and our coming in at unseasonable hours. Thou hast carried us through much labour of body, and much anxiety of mind. Thou hast blest in no common degree our unworthy labours in Thy cause ; Thou hast in some degree owned our endeavours.'

During this time Hannah More suffered frequently from violent attacks of pain in the head, which laid her quite aside from all active employments. Her testimony recorded in her diary in regard to these seasons of illness is useful in helping to do away with the too common idea that illness in itself has any sanctifying power, or that the soul which in times of health lives apart from God, is raised in any way by suffering itself into nearness to Him. It is not in sickness and disease that those who live in habitual communion with God can best rise in faith and love to the joy of His presence ; and still less can bodily weakness and suffering become in and of themselves a source of spiritual life to those who in health have never offered themselves to God as a reasonable service.

CHAPTER XII.

ANOTHER trial, more severe even than bodily suffering, about this time passed like a dark cloud across the sunshine of popularity and fame which Hannah More had so long enjoyed.

Many instances of opposition to the work of Hannah More and her sisters in the neglected parishes of Mendip are recorded in 'Miss Patty More's Diary;' the ignorance of the farmers, and their desire to keep down the labouring class, and the jealousy of cold-hearted clergymen, who felt their slothfulness rebuked by the labours of the Misses More, and who in every earnest effort dreaded Methodism, combined to produce constantly irritating opposition to the attendance of the people at the evening readings, and of the children at the schools. Still, the patience and tact of Hannah More and her sisters overcame these difficulties for a time, and in spite of all, this work for God was unshaken by any of the efforts of man to overturn it. The ill-will, however, did not subside with the success of the work, but gathered strength and virulence; and at last it broke forth into open attacks upon the character and actions of the Misses More and the teachers they had engaged.

The leader in this persecution, for so it may be called, was the curate of Blagdon, that village the reformation of which was only undertaken at the earnest request of the church-wardens and leading parishioners, at a time when Hannah More felt they had already more in hand than they could accomplish. The attack began by a false accusation against the schoolmaster at Blagdon. Both Miss Patty and Miss Hannah More were in London at the time, and the charge against the teacher was communicated to them by the curate in what Miss Patty calls 'a short and impudent letter.' They consulted influential friends in London, and the whole was referred to Sir A. Elton, who judged the accusation to be false. Having cleared his character, it was thought better that the master should leave the school, and he went to Dublin to superintend large charitable institutions there. The school at Blagdon was then discontinued, for neither Hannah More nor her sister thought it right to carry it on in a parish the only resident clergyman of which was so strongly opposed to their work.

Not satisfied with putting a stop to the good work in his own parish, the curate of Blagdon now used every endeavour to stir up others to oppose the efforts of these two women to bring light and help to the poor. In addition to accusations made to the bishop and dean against the teaching in the schools and in Hannah More's 'Cheap Repository' Tracts, that it was fanatical and seditious, charges were brought against her character by private slander, 'which,' as her old biographer says, 'were so preposterous as to conduce only to the defeat and disgrace of the fabricators.'

But there is often a vitality in evil things, and outrageous and even absurd as these slanders were (originally invented

8

by the hostile foes of religion and light to serve their own ends), the whisper of them has still hardly died away in some quarters, and they are occasionally repeated by persons who have never read the 'Mendip Annals,' nor the complete vindication which Hannah More's life and works establish.

During the time that she was undergoing this persecution, she was also suffering from an ague, which lasted seven months, and which was brought on by her constant devotion to the cause of the religious reformation and elevation of the lower classes. For herself, Hannah More determined to enter into no contest with her opponents, but to continue the work as God should make the way plain before them. To the Bishop of Bath and Wells alone did she write to explain her plans of teaching, and the subjects taught in her schools, holding herself in regard to him accountable for her conduct, 'which,' as she says, 'has been attacked with a wantonness of cruelty which, in civilized places, few persons, especially of my sex, have been called to suffer.'

'When I settled in this country thirteen years ago, I found the poor in many of the villages sunk in a deplorable state of ignorance and vice. There were, I think, no Sunday schools in the whole district, except one in my own parish, which had been established by our respectable rector, and another in the adjoining parish of Churchill. This drew me to the more neglected villages, whose distance made it very laborious. Not one school there did I ever attempt to establish without the hearty concurrence of the clergyman of the parish. My plan of instruction is extremely simple and limited. They learn, on week-days, such coarse work as may fit them for servants. I allow of no writing for the poor. My object is not to make fanatics, but to train up the lower classes in habits of industry and piety. I know no way of teaching morals but by teaching principles : or of inculcating Christian principles without imparting a good knowledge of Scripture. I own I have laboured this point diligently. My sisters and I always teach them ourselves every Sunday, except during our absence in the winter. By being out thirteen hours, we have generally contrived to visit two schools the same day, and to carry them to their respective churches. When we had more schools, we commonly visited them on a Sunday. The only books we use in teaching are two little tracts called "Questions for the Mendip Schools" (to be had of Hatchard), the "Church Catechism" (these are framed, and half a dozen hung up in the room); the Catechism, broken into short questions; Spelling Books, Psalter, Common Prayer, Testament, Bible. The little ones repeat "Watts's Hymns." The Collect is learned every Sunday. They generally learn the Sermon on the Mount, with many other chapters and psalms. Finding that what the children learned at school they commonly lost at home by the profaneness and ignorance of their parents, it occurred to me in some of the larger parishes to invite the latter to come at six on the Sunday evening, for an hour, to the school, together with the elder scholars. A plain printed sermon and a printed prayer is read to them, and a psalm is sung. I am not bribed by my taste—for, unluckily, I do not delight in music—but observing that singing is a help to devotion in others, I thought it right to allow the practice.

'For many years I have given away annually nearly two hundred Bibles, Common Prayer Books, and Testaments. To teach the poor to read, without providing them with *safe* books, has always appeared to me an improper measure, and this consideration induced me to enter upon the laborious undertaking of the "Cheap Repository" Tracts.

'In some parishes where the poor are numerous, such as Cheddar, and the distressed mining villages of Shipham and Rowbarrow, I have instituted, with considerable expense to myself, friendly benefit societies for poor women, which have proved a great relief to the sick and lying-in, especially in the late seasons of scarcity. We have in one single parish an accumulation of between two and three hundred pounds (the others in proportion); this I have placed out in the Funds. The late lady of the manor of Cheddar, in addition to her kindness to my institutions there, during her life, left, at her death, a legacy for the club, and another for the school, as a testimony to her opinion of the utility of both. We have two little annual festivities for the children and poor women of these clubs, which are always attended by a large concourse of gentry and clergy.

'At one of these public meetings Mr. Bere declared that since the

8—2

institution of the schools he could now dine in peace : for that where he used to issue ten warrants, he was not now called on for two.

'I shall take the liberty of sending your lordship the rules of my school, which have never been altered, and of referring you to the testimonials (printed in the public papers) of the churchwardens and principal inhabitants of some of those parishes where my conduct has been most attacked, to ascertain whether I have been used to act in concert with the minister, and whether my schools have been of any use in improving morals, or attracting the people to church.

'My schools were always honoured with the full sanction of the late bishop ; of which I have even recent testimonials. It does not appear that any one person who has written against them, except Mr. Bere, ever saw them. I am not accustomed to refer to others for my character ; I am not accustomed to vindicate it myself ; but it is natural to wish that it should not be taken from avowed enemies, or total strangers. My friendships and connections have not been among the suspected part of mankind. My attachment to the Established Church is, and has ever been, entire, cordial, inviolable, and, until now, unquestioned. Its doctrines and discipline I equally approve. I have long had the honour of reckoning many of its most distinguished dignitaries amongst my friends.

'I am too deeply sensible of the infirmity and evil of my own mind not to allow readily that much error and imperfection may have been mixed with my attempts to do a little good. But it would be false humility not to say that the whole drift and tendency has been right to the very best of my power. Mine is so far a singular case, that I not only feel myself guiltless of the motives and actions imputed to me, but I am conscious that all my little strength has been employed in the very contrary direction. Your lordship's enlightened mind will give me credit for studiously abstaining from what would, with ordinary judges, have best served my cause ; I mean a resentful retaliation on the conduct and motives of my adversaries.

'In one of the principal pamphlets against me, it is asserted that my writings *ought to be burned by the hands of the common hangman.* In most of them it is affirmed that my principles and actions are corrupt and mischievous in no common degree. If the grosser crimes alleged against me be true, I am not only unfit to be allowed to teach poor children to read, but I am unfit to be tolerated in any class of society. If, on the contrary, the heavier charges should prove not to be true, may it not furnish a presumption that the less are equally unfounded ? There is scarcely any motive so pernicious, nor any hypocrisy so deep, to which my plans have not been attributed ; yet I have neither improved my interest nor my fortune by them. I am not of a sex to expect preferment, nor of a temper to court favour ; nor was I so ignorant of mankind as to look for praise by a means so little calculated to obtain it ; though, perhaps, I did not reckon on such a degree of obloquy. If vanity were my motive, it has been properly punished ; if hypocrisy, I am hastening fast to answer for it at a tribunal, compared with which all human opinion weighs very light indeed ; in view of which the sacrifice which I have been called to make of health, peace, and reputation shrinks into nothing.'

Of her sister Patty at this time she writes: ' Poor Patty, in bad health herself, fights *manfully*, and combats well with these sorrows. She is holding our annual club feast, and feasting six or seven hundred each day with outward cheerfulness. It puts me in mind of poor actors, who play their comic parts gaily on the stage, when perhaps they have all sorts of miseries at home.' And in another letter : ' Patty behaves nobly, and only works the harder for all these attacks. She has been in all this weather on a three days' mission to Wedmore, where things look very smiling.'

This trial called forth strong expressions of sympathy from Hannah More's friends, many of whom were amongst the best and wisest of their time. Old John Newton writes : ' My dear madam, " blessed are ye when men shall revile and persecute you, and *shall speak all manner of evil against you falsely*, for My sake." When I consider whose words are these, I am more disposed to congratulate than to condole with you on the unjust and hard treatment you have met with. Yet I do feel for you. These things are not joyous, but grievous at the time ; yet cheer up, my dear friend, tarry thou the Lord's leisure. Be strong, and He shall comfort

thy heart.   Depend upon it, all shall turn out to the further-
ance of that Gospel for which you are engaged.'

Another letter Hannah More received at this trying time
was from the Duchess of Gloucester.   For some years now
she had been endeavouring to turn the intercourse she had
with persons of rank, who admired her works and enjoyed
her society, to good account for the service of God and
themselves.   In her diary for 1798 she wrote while in London,
' Had a little serious talk with the Duchess of Gloucester,
Lady Amherst, and the Duchess of Beaufort.   Lord, let me
be no mean respecter of persons, but make me valiant always
for Thy truth.'

At an earlier date she speaks of an evening spent at
Gloucester House as ' the most rational and religious evening
by far that I have passed in town.   It would make some folks
smile to know that we read the Epistle to the Ephesians, and
commented as we went along.'

A letter from the Duchess of Gloucester, written to Miss
Patty More during the time of the attacks made upon her
and her sister, and while Hannah More was suffering from
illness, shows the esteem in which she was held by the
princess :

' DEAR MADAM,

            ' The Bishop of London told me yesterday that
Miss H. More was very unwell.   Her life is of too much
consequence to the world not to create serious alarm to her
friends when she is indisposed ; but I very much fear that
she is at present very much more than indisposed.   Will you,
my dear Miss Martha, write me a few consolatory lines ? for
I am really very uneasy about her.   My reverence for her

unblemished character and exalted piety has turned into respectful affection ; and that she may be restored to us is the anxious prayer of, dear Miss Martha More,

'Your sincerely attached well-wisher,

'MARIA.

'My Sophia is, you may be certain, as anxious as myself.'

Other letters from Wilberforce, the Bishop of Bath and Wells, the Bishop of Durham, the Rev. Richard Cecil, and Mrs. Kennicott, consoled and supported the sisters during this trial.

On Hannah More's recovery, she and her sister Patty paid a visit to the Bishop of London at Fulham. Of this visit Miss Patty More thus writes to her sisters : 'We arrived here Thursday afternoon, and found Mrs. Kennicott, who has just been reading to us a sweet letter from Mrs. Barrington. She says, " So Hannah More has again been persecuted ; but she will indeed receive our Saviour's blessing, ' Blessed are they which are persecuted for righteousness' sake.'" Our friends say these trials will have a good ending, even in this world. Nothing can exceed, and few things equal, the behaviour of the bishop and Mrs. Porteus. I cannot express to you the very marked attentions which are paid to Hannah from all ranks and descriptions of people ; they say such a persecution of such a woman is unexampled.'

The attacks on Hannah More extended beyond the Mendip Hills ; scurrilous pamphlets were published against her in Bath, the 'Anti-Jacobin' directed its satire against her, and repeated a slander which gave amusement to herself and her sisters, and made her say to Mr. Wilberforce, 'I am sorry you do not read the 'Anti-Jacobin,' because you would have seen how I am in love with an actor and two officers at once.' The writer was probably not aware that she was then in her sixtieth year. But the 'Anti-Jacobin' afterwards changed its tone towards her, on the complete falseness of all the accusations against her becoming better known.

It was about this time that Hannah More and her sisters took to themselves the title of Mrs. instead of Miss, and requested their friends to address them thus. At a somewhat earlier time all ladies past their youth were addressed by the more dignified title, and they wished, perhaps, thus to mark their arrival at more advanced years.

In the meantime the schools which slander had endeavoured to damage flourished more and more. The people themselves learnt to feel the worth of them, the attendance increased, and improvements were made in the system and teaching as the new experience advanced. So far from being daunted or turned aside from this good work, the sisters devoted themselves with increasing earnestness and a deeper endeavour to reach the very heart of the people, and sow there the good seed of the kingdom of God—life and hope in Jesus Christ. With no symptom of fear, or thought of turning back from the work, they fully realized the motto of Miss Patty's journal of the 'Mendip Annals'—'I have not imitated Xenophon.'

CHAPTER XIII.

BARLEY WOOD.

THE persecution raised against Hannah More and her sisters extended over a period of more than two years ; during that time she removed from her cottage at Cowslip Green to a house she had built in a better situation, called Barley Wood. This was a larger and more convenient residence, and her sisters now gave up their house in Bath, and joined her in her new home. Here they all lived together until one after another of the four sisters gently passed to her home in heaven, leaving Hannah More alone. The house was cheerful and healthy, and the taste of the sisters was constantly at work in planting and cultivating the garden, and in carrying out various little plans for adding to the beauty of their rest-ing-place. One of their designs was to place among the trees memorial urns, in remembrance of departed friends or favourite authors.

A large number of persons visited them there, and Hannah More's extensive circle of correspondents kept them acquainted with all the ideas and events of the time.

Another branch of Hannah More's literary work at this time shows how fully she lived in her age, if not indeed before it. This is the series of books bearing on the education of women. We have seen how she was one of the first to recognise the right of the labouring classes to education and development, and she was also one of the first women to claim for women an education, the purpose of which should be individual culture, directed to the training of every faculty, so that the result might be a nobler and sweeter development more fit for the true work of life.

As early as 1799 she brought out her 'Strictures on Female Education,' the opening words of which are : 'It is a singular injustice which is exercised towards women, first to give them a very defective education, and then to expect from them the most undeviating conduct ; to train them in such a manner as shall lay them open to the most dangerous faults, and then censure them for not proving faultless, and for turning out that very kind of character for which it would be evident to an unprejudiced bystander that the whole scope and tenour of their instruction had been systematically preparing them.' From this it will be seen that she perceived how far the aim of the education of the day was lowered from the true ideal of womanhood, and had become a hindrance to its realization.

The education of that time had for its object mere external adornment and display. It consisted of a few showy accomplishments, taught for the purpose of exciting admiration. 'If,' says Hannah More, 'we were required to condense the reigning system of the brilliant education of a lady into an aphorism, it might be comprised in this short sentence—" *To allure and to shine.*" ' She then shows that a course of training with no higher purpose is not an education at all ; and sets forward a scheme of study in which the reasoning faculty is to be cultivated by books such as ' Watts's or Duncan's little books of Logic, some parts of Mr. Locke's " Essay on the

Human Understanding," and Bishop Butler's "Analogy." '
History is to be studied, so as to understand its principles and
lessons, and not as a 'mere collection of facts and anecdotes,
dates and epochs.' In like manner geography and natural
history are to be made the means of awakening intelligence,
observation, and giving a sense of the oneness of the human
family. The study of philology is advised as giving care in
exact use of words, and in clearly defining ideas and feelings,
instead of indulging in loose statements, exaggerated expressions of emotion, and vague ideas, all tending to untruthfulness.
The whole of the chapter on ' Definitions' would bear repetition
in the present day.

Considerable space is given to the subject of the culture of
the imagination and taste, in the education of women, by
accustoming girls to read the best works of poetry and fiction,
excluding carefully all that are false in sentiment and morals.
Amongst the means of promoting superficiality of mind, Mrs.
More justly places 'the swarms of abridgments, " Beauties,"
and compendiums of literature,' read or learnt by heart, with
no knowledge of the works themselves or their authors, and
which are no substitute for that true study of literature which
is one of the most important instruments in forming the
character of a woman.

Two great hindrances to the thorough culture which should
develop the whole character and faculties in a woman were
the time spent in learning music, and the means employed in
acquiring skill in speaking French.

Under the first Hannah More quotes the calculation of a
' person of great eminence now married to a man who dislikes
music.' From the age of six to eighteen she had spent four
hours a day 'in the acquisition of music,' making a total of

14,400 hours employed in learning an art which supplied her mind with no information nor ideas, and which she now never practised either for her own pleasure or that of others.

With great good sense Hannah More also estimates the value attached to French conversation at its true worth, and shows how, for an acquirement frequently of little use, 'piety and principle were offered up as victims to sounds and accents.' Why should Englishwomen, she asks, sacrifice so much to be able to converse with a nation who had done little of late to make their society desirable or improving? and why should an Englishwoman be ambitious of speaking French like a native, or of having it supposed she had been brought up in France? 'Some recent events may surely serve to reconcile an intelligent, well-educated Englishwoman to the suspicion of having been bred in her own country, and conversed more frequently in her own tongue.'

On the subject of objections brought against the fuller education of women, from the idea of its rendering them ambitious of power, and unfit for the duties of life, Hannah More says:

'The more a woman's understanding is improved, the more obviously will she discern that there can be no happiness in any society where there is a perpetual struggle for power; and the more her judgment is rectified, the more accurate views will she take of her true life and its duties, and the more readily will she accommodate herself to them; it is the *most vulgar and ill-informed women who are ever most inclined to be domestic tyrants;* and those always struggle most vehemently for power who feel themselves at the greatest distance from deserving it, and who would not fail to make the worst use of it when attained. An uneducated woman is far more masculine than one in whom all the graces of intellect, the delicate vibrations of feeling, and the refinements of taste have been duly recognised and cultivated. Co-operation, and not competition, is the clear principle we wish to see reciprocally adopted by those higher minds in each sex which really approximate the nearest to each other.'

Hannah More's old friends, Mrs. Carter, Mrs. Chapone, Mrs. Barbauld, and Mrs. Montagu, all of them ladies who had made self-improvement an earnest purpose in their lives, welcomed warmly Hannah More's book; but the age was scarcely ripe for its general reception, and probably one witty lady was right when she said, 'Everybody will read her, everybody admire her, and *nobody mind her.*' Old John Newton's shrewd sense saw at once the truth in Hannah More's views, and he writes to her after reading the 'Strictures on Female Education:'

' I thank the Lord for disposing and enabling you to write it, and my heart prays that it may be much read, and that the blessing of the Lord may accompany the perusal, and make it extensively useful, answering to your design and far beyond your expectation.'

A few years after the publication of the 'Strictures on Female Education,' Hannah More wrote ' Hints towards forming the Character of a Young Princess.' It was brought out anonymously in 1805, just at the time that the question of a suitable education for the Princess Charlotte, heiress to the throne, was being discussed. Mrs. Hannah More's intimacy with the Duchess of Gloucester had given her frequent interviews with the young princess, and she had formed a high opinion of her talents. Just as Hannah More had finished her work, the Bishop of Exeter, Dr. Fisher, was appointed the tutor of the princess, and to him therefore she sent the book. The bishop wrote to her, highly approving her views for the princess's education, he addressing her as a man, and a correspondence, in which she preserved her incognito, was carried on between them. A copy of the book was presented by the bishop to the Queen, who highly approved of it, and desired to know if Mrs. Hannah More were not the author, as she traced resemblance in it to her earlier work on female education. The secret soon became known, and Hannah More received many letters from the nearer relatives of the princess thanking her for the work.

Her next work was of an altogether new character. In her 'Strictures on Female Education' she had recommended fiction as one means of cultivating the imagination; but there were few novels fit for the purpose, and some of her friends thought she had done wrong in advising their use at all in the education of a young girl. Some of these remarks, perhaps, suggested to her the idea of writing a novel which should be designed especially for girls, and which might exhibit in action some of her views in regard to the education of women. The heroine was to be the ideal woman, as daughter, sister, and wife; and further to illustrate her ideas, various other characters, in whom might be shown the evil results of the prevailing false system of education, were also to be introduced. She called her novel 'Cœlebs in Search of a Wife.'

It was published in December, 1809, in two volumes, and excited so much attention that in a few days a second edition was called for, and before the end of a fortnight it was out of print. During the next twelve months, no less than twelve editions were published, and its popularity continued during the lifetime of its author. In America it ran through thirty editions within a few years. Like many of Hannah More's works, 'Cœlebs' was published anonymously ; but she was so well known in such a large circle, that her style of writing was recognised immediately by all her intimate friends, and the secret was soon spread abroad. After paying all expenses of publication, and the bookseller's profits, Mrs. Hannah More cleared £2,000 by the work during the first twelve-month. The price of the book was 12s.

The success of 'Cœlebs' must be partly attributed to its being the first book of its kind, for while passing as a novel, it was also recognised as a religious work, having a very serious purpose. Compared with many a fiction equally high in aim, but full of life and feeling, 'Cœlebs' would in the present day scarcely find a reader. Hannah More was no more a novelist than she was a dramatist, but she was a skilful writer, and had seen a good deal of society, so that her sketches of character are fair representations of many of the social types of the time ; but she is far more interested in pressing her own views upon various subjects, and in correcting the evils of society, than she is in the men and women of her story. These are not living creations, but mere illustrations of her religious and social opinions.

The plan of the story is simple enough. Cœlebs has lost his father and mother ; he is lonely, and wishes for a wife. He sets out to pay a round of visits to his friends, and he hopes among them to find the lady he wants as a companion for life. 'I do not want a Helen,' he says to himself, as he drives along in his post-chaise, 'nor a St. Cecilia, nor a Madame Dacier : yet she must be elegant, or I should not love her ; sensible, or I should not respect her ; prudent, or I could not confide in her ; well-informed, or she could not train my children ; well bred, or she could not entertain my friends ; consistent, or I should offend the shade of my mother ; pious, or I should not be happy with her.' He goes first to London. Here he visits a gentleman, a widower, with two pretty daughters. The arrangements of the house and table are so bad that Cœlebs concludes the ladies are wholly occupied in higher intellectual pursuits. He therefore asks them ' if they did not think Virgil the finest poet in the world ?' but they stare, and declare they never before had heard of him ; they are wholly ignorant and uneducated, ' and,' says Cœlebs, ' I rose from the table with a full conviction that it is very possible for a woman to be totally ignorant of the duties of common life without knowing one word of Latin, and that her being a bad companion is no proof of being a good economist.'

The next visit was to a Mr. Ranby, at Hampstead, who had a reputation as an eminently religious man. Mrs. Ranby's time was occupied in attending meetings, and running after her favourite preachers. There are here two daughters, whom she has totally neglected, being satisfied with the fact that they had never been to a ball or play in their lives, and that she never allowed them to read any books which were not religious. These young ladies are empty-headed and frivolous in the extreme. They spend their days ' in playing the piano and harp, in copying some indifferent drawings, gilding a set of flower-pots, and netting white gloves and veils.' Mrs. Ranby stands as the type of the narrow, self-righteous religionist, satisfied with holding certain doctrines, and regarding the teaching of Christ as ' not to be taken literally.'

At Lady Belfield's Cœlebs meets with some fashionable

young ladies of the day, whose actions are all studied for
effect, and with Lady Bab Lawless, who represents the fast
woman of that time. Here also he is introduced to Lady
Denham, who, it being Passion Week, has before her in the
room where she receives visitors a large book, called 'A
Week's Preparation.' She abstains from certain fixed amusements during the holy season, ' but indemnified herself for her
abstinence from her usual diversions by indulging in the only
pleasures which she thought compatible with the sanctity of
the season—*uncharitable* gossip and unbounded calumny.' As
her friends are leaving, she says, '*I am sorry* this is a week in
which I cannot see my friends at their assemblies, but on
Sunday, you know, it will be all over, and I shall have my
house full in the evening.'

From London, and the various characters represented in its
society, Cœlebs passes on to visit at the house of a Mr.
Stanley in Hampshire. Hitherto Cœlebs has of course met
with no lady whom he would like to ask to be his wife; but
Mr. Stanley has two daughters, and Lucilla, the elder, represents Hannah More's ideal of what a young lady should be.
Cœlebs thus describes her :

' Lucilla Stanley is rather perfectly elegant than perfectly
beautiful. I have seen women as striking, but I never saw
one so interesting ; it is not so much the symmetry of features
as *the joint triumph of intellect and sweet temper.* A fine old
poet has well described her :

> " Her pure and eloquent blood
> Spoke in her cheeks, and so distinctly wrought,
> That one could almost say her body thought !"

Her conversation is full of liveliness, sensibility, and delicacy.
There is nothing like effort in her expression, or vanity in her

manner. She has rather a playful gaiety than a pointed wit.
Taste is indeed the predominating quality of her mind, and
she may rather be said to be a nice judge of genius in others
than to be a genius herself. The same true feeling pervades
her writing, her conversation, her dress, her domestic arrangements. Though she has a correct ear she neither sings nor
plays. Her notions are too just to allow her to be satisfied
with mediocrity, and for perfection in art she thinks life is too
short, without neglecting the culture of the mind and other
various and important duties.' Sir John Belfield says of
Lucilla later, 'What a refreshment it is to see a girl of fine
sense more cultivated than accomplished, the creature not of
music, dancing, and French masters, but of nature, of books,
and of good company !'

It will be thus seen that Hannah More illustrates in Lucilla
the ideas she had already brought forward in the 'Strictures
on Female Education,' that the best life and development of
women is attained by culture rather than by so-called accomplishments. Later in the story she again takes up the evil of
the large amount of time spent in acquiring mechanical skill
in playing on the piano, and in facility in speaking French ;
neither of which arts touches the mind, nor gives it any knowledge or culture that is fruitful in after-life, or that fits a
woman for her true work in the home or in society. Hannah
More was one of the first writers to perceive this, and to point
it out ; but when ideas are fixed by fashion, and followed
through subservience to it, it takes long for sense and judgment to gain ground ; and it is only in this generation that
the idea is fully received of choosing in the education of
women those subjects for study which train the mind and
form the taste, giving depth and fulness to the inner life.

CHAPTER XIV.

INNER LIFE—DIARY, 1803, 1804.

HANNAH MORE renewed again, during the progress of 1803, her secret controversy with her own heart, and her solemn pledges of service in the work of edification and practical piety. Her diary of this year presents to us the mirror of a mind gathering strength daily from the increasing conviction of its natural weakness, and from the succours of grace conceded to prayer and self-abasing confession before the throne of grace.

She commences it in the following terms :

'*January* 1, 1803.—Since I have been in some measure drawn off from the pursuits of the world, and have laboured, though in a most imperfect manner, to assist others in the knowledge of the truth—my life being active and my health bad, I find I have neglected my writing ; but being now, through the will of God, brought to a life of more leisure and retirement, I resolve, through grace, to resume it. And do Thou, O Lord, grant that I may be more fixed in my thoughts, more frequent in self-examination, more heedful of the emotions of my own mind, more mindful of death, from thus marking the progress to it. O Lord, I resolve to begin this year with a solemn dedication of myself to Thee : Thine I am ; I am not my own ; I am bought with a price. Let the time past suffice for me to have lived in the world—let me henceforward live to Him who loved me and gave Himself for me. Lord, do Thou sanctify to me my long and heavy trials. Let them not be removed till they have answered those ends which they were sent to accomplish.

'*January* 5.—I fear I am become more intent on reading Scripture and cultivating retirement, than willing to bestow time on others. I have hitherto erred on the other side ; the danger now is, lest the slanders I have met with should drive me to too much caution and silence.

'*January* 7.—Various trials, acting on a nervous frame and keenly feeling temper, have disturbed my peace and health—I fear to the discredit of religion. Blessed be God, my mind is not only placable, but is become serene. Instead of being disturbed by every petty event, I now endeavour not to think very much of anything which is to end when this life ends.

'*January* 8.—Have been frequent in prayer for poor Mr. ——, who is supposed to be dying ; Lord, lay not to his charge his offences against me. I forgive him, as I hope to be forgiven.

'*Sunday*, *January* 9.—Formerly I was glad when they said unto me, "Let us go up into the house of our God." Now I endeavour to submit cheerfully to be detained by sickness from church ; yet it is a great hindrance to spiritual improvement, and I ascribe it partly to this, that I have scarcely ever known any one person who has lived long abroad retain much serious piety. Lord, I thank Thee that my lot was cast in a land of light and knowledge, where the name of Christ is publicly professed, and Christianity preached in its purity. I bless Thee for Thy day, Thy Word, Thy Spirit. Lord, grant that my advantages may not one day appear against me ; and that while strangers are called from the north and the south, from the east and the west, I, with all my means, may not be shut out of Thy kingdom.

'*January* 10.—Heard to-day of fresh persecution ; new attacks from the old quarter ; after frequent promises of silence. Lord, grant that I may bear this with a holy resignation to Thy will. If reputation be the sacrifice Thou requirest, Thy will be done. I try daily to look less to human applause, and more to Thy favour, which is eternal life. Grant that I may not be content with *saying* this ; do Thou enable me to *do* it.

'*January* 12.—Finished reading "Halyburton's Life." It is so ill written, so full of Scottish idioms and vulgarisms, and so uncouth, that, together with the gloomy state of his mind, it was a heavy labour to get through the first half ; but the second made rich amends ; it exhibits the most consolatory view of a soul which had struggled with and conquered habitual sin ; all ending in such a vigorous unshaken faith, and such a triumphant death-bed, as must animate the coldest heart, and leave the most cheering impression of the truth of Christianity.

'*January* 13.—I was struck at hearing read one of my own stories, "'Tis all for the best!" meant as an answer to Voltaire's ridicule of optimism. The story goes strongly to the vindication of every dispensation of Providence, and inculcates unqualified submission in the warmest terms. I blushed to think that I had not acted up to my own views—"'Thou that teachest another, teachest not thou thyself!'"

'*January* 19.—A delightful letter from my dear ancient friend. Mrs. Boscawen, at eighty-four : her praise of me too exalted, but kindly meant to support me under my strange attack. She desires my prayers ; how many do this, who little know how much more I need theirs, and what a poor, erring, sinful creature I am !

'*January* 20.—I try to bring into practice this remark. If I get repentance by affliction, it is not so much a trouble as an advantageous traffic ; it is a voyage which has pain in the way, but treasure in the end. No affliction can hurt him that is penitent and believing ; if we escape, it will make us more thankful ; if not, it will bring us nearer to God.

'*January* 24.—Seeing that evils which I feared have been graciously withheld, and mercies which I despaired of have been granted, I would learn to trust God more, to commit myself to Him, to throw aside all anxiety, and neither to fear remote evils, nor to look for distant good.

'*January* 25.—With sorrow I find, that though it has pleased God by various trials, both in my health and fame, to wean me from what is called the world ; and I have, through grace, obtained a considerable deadness to honours, pleasure, and human applause, yet it is easy to detect the same spirit still at work on nearer occasions, and in the daily petty affairs of life. I am discomposed by trifles which I despise, and feel inequalities of temper at trifling faults in others ; am impatient at their follies, weaknesses, imprudences; forgetting how often I myself offend, not only against them, but against infinite mercy and inexhaustible patience. Blessed be God for Jesus Christ !

'*January* 27.—I am thankful to say that my thoughts in the night. in which my waking hours are many, are for the most part on serious subjects ; but I grieve to find, that though my reins chasten me in the night season, yet when the light of day restores cheerfulness and gaiety, and objects are alive about me, I cannot get back altogether to that spirituality which the night encouraged.

'*January* 28.—I find it hard, nay impossible, to acquit myself during the day of the promises and resolutions made in the night season : this furnishes fresh, constant reasons for flying "to the fountain open for sin and uncleanness ;" it serves to keep the heart humble, by showing its constant need of pardon, mercy, and the pleading of the Divine Intercessor.

'*February* 2.—My birthday ! How slender was my prospect this day twelvemonth that I should live to see it ! I would enumerate some of the mercies of the past year : Raised up from a long and dangerous sickness —from a broken state of nerves and spirits, restored to a serene and re- signed frame of mind, able to thank God, not only for amended health and spirits, for the many comforts and alleviations of my long and heavy trial, but enabled to thank Him for the trial itself : it has shown me more of the world, more of its corruptions, more of my own heart, more of the instability of human opinion ; and it has weaned me from many attach- ments which were too strong to be right. Among other mercies, I have been preserved from injury, when my horse twice fell under me. My schools are not only continued, but God has raised up a powerful protector in the new bishop. He has enabled me to meet, without resentment, those whom I knew to be my enemies. He has given me a new and de- lightful habitation, and continued to me many friends : " Bless the Lord, O my soul !" May I seriously renew my repentance for the sins of the past year, and enter upon a new course of holy obedience. I would also reckon it among my mercies that I have escaped the bustle and worldliness of a Bath winter, and have so much time at my disposal. Oh that I could spend it to the glory of the great Giver !

'*February* 6.—In the night I had much comfortable intercourse with my heavenly Father, and felt resigned to His will, whether it decreed that I should pass through honour or dishonour, evil report or good report, life or death ; but when the business of the day returns, the unsteadiness of my own heart, and the frivolous conversation of others sadly diminish these good impressions. Oh for more permanent spirituality of mind !

'*February* 17.—A sleepless night, but, I thank God, no great pain. I did not indulge my gloomy thoughts : nor did lamenting recollections obtain power over my mind, but I was enabled to repeat larger passages of Scripture, and to pray.

'*February* 18.—Another month has passed over my head. I have to be thankful for its mercies. No calamity hath befallen, nor any evil over- taken me, but such as is common, and to be expected in a life frail, un- certain, and suffering. Oh for warmer aspirations after a life that shall have no sorrow and no end !

'*February* 27.—I am grieved to find on this Sunday, that though I have leisure, I have not the right relish for serious objects. I find it impossible, alas! to confine my thoughts to any devout contemplations for any length of time. "Who shall deliver me from this body of death and sin?" I thank my God through Jesus Christ, that my mind kept up a sense of devotion for a blessed interval on first awaking this morning.

'*March* 2.—This day finished Paley's "Natural Theology." It is a very able work—evinces the author's acquaintance with anatomy, and almost all science. All these endowments are made subservient to the grand purpose for which the book is written. But the work is still deficient in some essential points.

'*March* 12.—Poor Captain —— has been spending some days with us. I think it has pleased God, by the trial of his sickness, to work a material change in his heart. There seems to be in him a growing delight in spiritual things, and a tenderness of conscience. I bless Thee, Lord, that that exemplary servant of Thine, his sergeant, was one of our first scholars at Cheddar, and that Thou hast graciously preserved him in faith and virtue, in a station so full of temptation. With Thy grace a camp may become a sanctuary, and without it the holiest place may be converted into a scene of iniquity.

'*March* 15.—Finished this day, for the second time, Bishop Horne's "Paraphrase of the Psalms." A work of great edification, and of a sweet and devout spirit. I do not know any book that has greater unction and savour of piety. Only one thing surprises me, that this excellent man falls into the common error of mistaking baptism for regeneration. Surely it is confounding the outward and visible sign with the inward and spiritual grace.

'*March* 24.—I feel in finishing my garden that I have too much anxiety to make it beautiful; that it occupies too much of my attention, and tends to give worldly thoughts a predominance in my mind. How imperfection mixes itself with all we do and are! This innocent relaxation, which Providence seems kindly to have provided for me so seasonably in the time of my distress and depression, is in danger of becoming a snare, by fixing me too much to that world from which I am in other respects trying to free myself. May I ever remember, that whatever keeps the mind from God, or that stops the heart short of heavenly things, however harmless in itself, becomes sinful by drawing the time and thoughts and affections from their proper and legitimate objects. I have, perhaps, too strong a passion for scenery and landscape-gardening.

'*Sunday, March* 27.—By the great favour and goodness of God, I have this day been enabled to go to church. Adored be Thy holy Name, that I am again restored to this privilege. Oh may it be sanctified to me! May I lift up my heart in gratitude for every spiritual blessing--for Sabbaths, for ordinances, for ministers! May I be less unfruitful under these multiplied advantages! Every opportunity increases my responsibility. Let me always remember that it was to the *professors*, to the *instructed*, to those who, because they had the *means*, made sure of salvation, that the Lord said, "Depart from Me, I never knew you." Better to have been a pagan, a blind, ignorant idolater, than a disobedient Christian, or an unfruitful believer.

'*Good Friday.*—May the awful transactions of this holy day sink deep into my heart, and may I resolve with more effect than I have hitherto done to live henceforth to Him who died for me. May all my reading and meditation this day respect that great event on which my own salvation and that of the whole world depends. Lord Jesus, hasten Thy great work, and grant that the knowledge of Thee may cover the earth, as the waters cover the sea. Bring in the Gentiles, convert Thine ancient people the Jews, and finally accomplish the number of Thine elect.

'*April* 13.—A fresh call to repentance and preparation, in the death of one of my oldest friends, Mr. L.——. Our acquaintance began when I was eighteen; we were both then devoted to poetry, literature, and intellectual amusement. His was a singular character. About the middle of life he renounced worldly society and reading, yet persisted in a close application to business. He fell into the habits and opinions of the mystics—was much given up to secret devotion, devout meditation, and a thoughtful intercourse with his Maker. I have no doubt of his sincerity, but he was a character rather to be admired than imitated. He left off at last all public worship. Taking no active part in society, he brought little glory to God, and was less useful to mankind than his talents, his virtues, and his fortune ought to have made him. He was, however, one of the most amiable, gentle, and self-denying of men, and with all his peculiarities, was, I doubt not, a sincere Christian *in his way*. May I be found watching, as I doubt not he was!

'*April* 19.—On Sunday I was enabled to go twice to church, through the goodness of God. Shipham in the morning; the first time of my visiting the schools. I hope I was thankful for being restored to my poor children, and for finding a very full and flourishing school, well-informed in the Scriptures. We can only put Christianity into their *heads:* do Thou, O Father of mercies ! put it into their *hearts*, and sanctify our labours !

'*April* 22.—Mr. Whalley passed a day or two with us. I am always edified by his highly devotional spirit. He seems more dead to the world, and to realize the invisible things of eternity more than almost any man I ever knew. We conversed much on serious subjects, and read largely in Bishop Reynolds. I have to lament that the impression of such reading and such conversation is so soon effaced. Last night, having lost my feverish symptoms, I was enabled to keep up devout thoughts and prayers during all my waking intervals. Oh that I could carry them more into the intercourse of the world !

'*May* 4.—Indisposition of body and mind has prevented my writing. Things the most trivial and contemptible occupy, distract, and indispose the soul for its proper work. I fear I have gone back in religion this week. My waking nightly thoughts have been less voluntarily pious. I find with sorrow that I stand in need of continual calls and awakening ; for when all goes on peacefully, I easily degenerate into sloth and deadness.

'*May* 5.—One ill consequence I experience from my long trial is, that whereas I used to watch for all occasions for introducing useful subjects, I am now backward to do it, from the idea that all I say may be called enthusiasm. Alas ! it is a difficult case—I know not how to act. Lord, direct me by Thy Spirit. The low tone, too, of common conversation is very unfavourable to a spirit of devotion. I seize, however, what time I can to be alone, and that is the time I most truly enjoy. I do not get weary of holy reading ; but meditation and prayer too soon fail. Just finished Hayley's " Life of Cowper." Cowper's letters are interesting, as they present to view the genuine, affectionate, benevolent heart of the incomparable author. I was disappointed to find so few of his religious letters printed. The biographer seems to forget, or not to know, that religion was the grand feature, the turning-point in the character of Cowper. It was difficult to write his life truly, and yet tenderly. Hayley has very judiciously sunk some circumstances which might have been misunderstood ; and he has treated his insanity with great tenderness. The whole is written in a good temper, and much favour is shown to religious people. As to the composition of the life, by way of preface, it is in a bad taste, florid and incorrect. It is, however, with all its faults, a pleasing work, but might have been made far more useful. The letters wind about the heart, and captivate the affections, by their natural feeling, truth, elegance, and simplicity.

'*June* 18.—A long pause. P. and I have been absent a month at Cheltenham to drink the waters. However I may be as to bodily improvement, I fear my soul has not prospered in health. With fewer impediments than I have almost ever had, fewer trials, more leisure for reading and meditation, I am not more spiritually-minded. I read with little improvement, I fear, though I read much. O Lord, do Thou root the spirit of worldliness out of my heart. It flourishes there, because it finds a congenial soil.

'*July* 20.—I had hung my harp upon the willows, never more to take it down, as I thought : but importunity on the one hand, and supineness on the part of others, have driven me to write a popular song on the dread of invasion. What a state of things must we be in, when the most immediate way of doing good that occurs, is for *me* to *write* a song ! I was driven to make it merrily loyal ; had it been serious it would have been scouted.

'*July* 29.—Heard to-day that my enemies had been undermining my character, among those of the highest rank. I am anew accused of disaffection to those whom my humble talents have heartily supported, and whom it is one great business of my life to support. Blessed be God ! I heard this with little emotion. Oh how thankful am I, that I can now hear such charges with patience ! May I more and more learn of Him who was meek and lowly ; may I with humble reverence reflect that even that Divine and Perfect Being was accused of sedition, and of stirring up the people.

'*September* 30.—I find it easier to pray that others may be weaned from the world than to be weaned myself. I have spent nearly all this week in my garden ; too much occupied by amusement without doors, and company within. I am now, through the mercy of my God, come to the conclusion of another month. Great have been my mercies—great my undeservings. I would especially be thankful for a letter from the Rev. ——, acknowledging the good done in his parish by my tracts—and to his own soul by one in particular—that on bringing religion into the common business of life. May my heart be filled with gratitude for that goodness which has vouchsafed to work by so worthless an instrument.

'*Sunday*.—We were all at Wrington church, and at sacrament. This last is a blessing I have so rarely enjoyed the last two years, that I cannot be thankful enough for any such opportunity. O Lord, hear and confirm the vows I offered up to Thee at Thy table ; strengthen my faith, animate my hope, influence my charity. I was not well ; I hope that may partly account for the coldness of my heart. When shall I be dead unto sin and alive unto God?

' *Tuesday night, October* 9.—At home for reading and prayer ; but a cold heart and dead affections. Lord, prepare every heart, and especially my own, to confess with deep contrition and self-abhorrence our great and numberless transgressions : and may we say in the view of our great military preparations, " Cursed is the man that trusteth in man, and maketh flesh his arm, and departeth from the living God."

' *October* 13.—What a miscellaneous world ! What different scenes occupy successive days ! Yesterday, Patty and I dined at Clevedon, to meet the Duke of ——, though our hearts were fresh bleeding with the recent wound of Drewitt's death. I thought it right to go, as a desire had been expressed for my acquaintance, which, under any other circumstances than those of my late trials, I should have thought of no importance. But neither the compliments nor the splendours of the day could make me forget my dear departed friend. We stayed all night.

' *Friday, October* 14.—My beloved friend, Mr. Wilberforce, and his family, came to pass a few days. I bless God that we were permitted to meet once more in this tempestuous world, in tolerable peace and comfort. I hope to profit by this fresh view of this excellent man's faith and holiness ; his superiority to worldly temptation and worldly censure ; his patience under provocations, and his lively gratitude for the common mercies of life.

' *Monday, October* 17.—After breakfast the Wilberforces departed for Bath, and Patty and I for Cheddar, to pay the last sad duty to Drewitt. When I saw the poor widow, there were no tears, no murmurs, no complaints, it was the most heroic piety and exemplary fortitude. We attended the widow with her three young children, to take her last leave of the body, before it was carried out of the house. She leaned in a praying posture for a long time over the coffin, embracing it—her little ones beside her—but not a groan escaped her ; she was solemnly silent, but her heart was praying.

' Mr. B—— preached a most interesting funeral sermon to above two thousand weeping auditors, and it fell to his hard lot to read the prayers, and to bury the friend of his heart. After sermon, the widow quietly walked out of her pew, took her babies by the hand, and went to the grave, over which she stood without indulging any emotion during the last sad ceremony. When all was over she walked with her children back to the house, to which the mournful procession all returned. The sight and sorrow of R——, the beloved friend of her husband, at length forced a flood of tears from this heroic mourner. If I am not the better for her example on this occasion, it will be among the number of my sins. Lord, sanctify to us all, and to me in particular, the solemnities of this day ; and grant that the sight of youth, genius, and virtue consigned to the grave, may quicken my preparation for it. Such were the last honours paid to an obscure country curate, whose talents and acquirements would have adorned the highest station ; but whose humility and piety eminently fitted him for that which he filled.

'*October* 20.—Yesterday, the 19th, was the public fast. It appears to have been not only decently but solemnly observed everywhere. O Lord, accept the prayers which Thy sinful, but in many instances, I trust, Thy repenting creatures, have offered up at the throne of Thy grace ; and grant that sorrow for sin may be an abiding principle in the hearts of all those whose lips yesterday confessed it. Accept the prayers which were offered up for our king and country. Avert the stroke which we have most righteously deserved ; and grant that, renouncing all dependence on ourselves and on an arm of flesh, we may place it solely on Thy tender mercies in Christ Jesus. Unite the hearts of this nation, as the heart of one man, both in their allegiance to the king, and especially to Thee the King of kings and Lord of lords ; and grant that whatever may be the event, we may be taught by it a deeper submission to Thy will ; and if in anger Thou hast decreed that national peace should be deferred, as a punishment for our sins, grant that we may individually have peace with Thee, through our Lord Jesus Christ.

'*November* 3.—We have had the comfort of two days of the company of our dear friend H. T. His mild, peaceful, subdued, holy, cheerful spirit does honour to religion. May God spare him to a world not worthy of him. I forgot to record that on nearly the same day with Drewitt, B—— was called away to answer at the bar of God for a life spent in opposition to the light of knowledge and education. He was one of the worst calumniators of poor D. Both called into eternity together ! Oh, how different the account they had to give of their respective talents !

'Some petty vexations from a friend convinced me too sadly how much I am still in the power of trifles, and how little, after all, the world is crucified to me and I to the world. Oh that I had the wings of a dove !

'*November* 29.—Being able to do little or nothing to serve our country, it occurred to us as a sacrifice it would become us to make that I should

write and offer to give up Barley Wood to the commanding officers at
Bristol, to be entirely at their disposal in the event of the French actually
landing at Uphill, eight miles distant ; or a partial use of our house in the
meanwhile ;—a kind letter of thanks and friendly refusal for the present,
but of acceptance in case of an invasion, has satisfied our minds that we
did right in making the offer.

'*Sunday*, 27*th of November.*—Too damp and wet for schools or church.
Tried to improve the solitude thus afforded me. Read " Baxter's Funeral
Sermon," and some of the more serious passages of his life, and found
them striking, and in some respects appropriate ; but how sadly do I fall
short of him, particularly where he speaks of his calumnious assailants.
Fifty books were written against *him ;* about twenty-three, I think, were
written *for* and against *me ;* besides three years' monthly attack from the
" Anti-Jacobin ;" but while Baxter blessed God that none of these things
disturbed him, I have to lament that through my want of his faith and
piety they had nearly destroyed my life. In one thing only I had the
advantage—I never once *replied* to my calumniators. In this one thing his
trial was less than mine—that his calumniators did not hinder him in the
service of God by diminishing his estimation as a writer, whereas I believe
that the false witness borne against me has caused my works to be much
less read and more condemned : but God can carry on His own work,
though all such poor tools as I were broken.

'*November* 29.—I am much more sensible than heretofore of the
breadth and length and depth of the radical sin of selfishness, and of the
excellence and necessity of self-denial and public spirit and charity.

'*November* 30.—Lord, grant me more patience and watchfulness, and
forgive my numberless sins, known and unknown, for the merits, and
sacrifice, and intercession of my Saviour Jesus Christ.

' I have been much humbled in reading an account of the death of good
Mr. K——'s son. What resignation to the Divine will, what trust in
Christ, what love of God *under* trials, and *for* trials, at the early age of
nineteen ! At three times that age, how cold, how dead, how slack am I
in preparation for that eternity which is so rapidly advancing.

'*December.*—Letter from Mr. Pearson declining Cheddar. This is a
great grief. Lord, let it be a sanctified grief. Teach me a complete
acquiescence in Thy holy will ; the work is in Thine hand ; to Thee I
would commit it. Deliver my soul from all sinful anxiety, and let me not
be anxious about *Thy* work, but my *own.* Oh for more faith in the promises, more renunciation of my own wisdom, my own will, my own way !

'*Sunday, December* 11.—Patty is gone to take leave of Shipham. It grieves me, whose health is better than hers, thus to put the labouring oar on her ; but the fear of being laid up for the winter deters me. I have spent this Sabbath morning in my own room, with much peace of mind ; I never do this voluntarily ; public worship is God's ordinance, and ought never to be omitted but on very strong grounds. Without public worship all private religion would soon decay.

'*December* 25.—In the midst of my pain I have secretly been trying to reconcile friends whom trifles had set at variance. Oh, what an imperfect world it is ! Good people quarrel for very nothings. For my own part I feel so much sinfulness in my own nature, that it makes me lenient to the faults of others. I say this now with more truth, from having felt sinful tempers rise in my mind to-day about trifles. Shall I not then forgive my fellow-sinner his hundred pence—I who have a debt of a thousand talents to be forgiven ? May we bear one another's burdens ; and may I prepare for that period of pain, and weariness, and imbecility, which must be found in that old age which is approaching.'

Her diary for 1804 is the last of those interesting impressions of her mind found among her papers, in which her thoughts flow in a consecutive series ; and which, while they indicate the progress of her self-searching piety, and its beautiful surrender to Divine discipline, exhibits an instructive specimen of the great gain of godliness, in the settled serenity and happy confidence in which it lands us at the last.

'*Sunday, January* 1, 1804.—I am now, through the great and undeserved mercy of my God, brought to the beginning of another Sunday and another year. "Bless the Lord, O my soul, and forget not all His benefits ; who forgiveth all thy sins and pardoneth all thine iniquities." O Lord, give me grace on this day solemnly and seriously to repent of the sins of my whole life, and especially of the sins which the past year has added to the sins of my former life. And do Thou touch my heart with a deep and lively sense of Thy continued, renewed, and increased mercies. Enable me this day to pass over in review these particular mercies ; among others, a considerable restoration of my health and spirits ; personal and family comforts continued ; family misfortunes averted ; opportunities of doing some good ; our schools continued ; kindness of friends ; ability to enjoy my sweet place ; escape from the turbulent life of Bath ; increased opportunities of reading and retirement. I have, too, to be thankful, amidst grievous alarms and dangers, for many public blessings ; for an unusual degree of domestic peace and unanimity ; for the cordiality with which all ranks have come forward in defence of the country ; that a foreign invasion has been mercifully kept off, and that we have had time for preparation. So blind and ignorant are we, that perhaps even those very winds and tempests which have made us tremble for our safety have helped to insure it. We know not, as to temporals, what we should ask for ; let me, therefore, implore earthly blessings with entire submission to the Divine will ; but in praying for spiritual mercies no reserve, no caution, no limitation is necessary. Lord, pour out the grace of Thy Holy Spirit on me and mine without measure ; teach us to love *Thee* with *all* our hearts, minds, souls, and strength, and to devote the remainder of our lives to Thy service, and to the glory of our Lord and Saviour Jesus Christ.

'*January* 7.—Intense pains in my head and face continue. Lord, give me more patience : "Shall a living man complain ?" Oh, how much fewer are my sufferings than my sins ; how much less do I suffer for my sins than my Saviour suffered for them !

'*January* 14.—Blessed be God for an interval of ease for two days. I call myself to account for my late deadness, and hardness, and worldliness, disturbed with petty cares, and my heart much alienated from prayer by those very sufferings which ought to have drawn my soul nearer to God. "Oh, wretched man that I am, who shall deliver me from the body of this death ? I thank God through Jesus Christ." A visit from Mr. A—— ; he declares that the country is in a complete state of defence, and the foe hourly expected. Lord, strengthen our arms and prepare our hearts. Alas ! what preparations are the great of my own sex making ! Balls, routs, masquerades ; such was the preparation Belshazzar made, when Cyrus burst the brazen gates, and Babylon was lost in a night. O Lord, awake this sinful, sleeping land. Death and eternity ! impress these two awful words on all our hearts.

'Mr. and Mrs. and Miss H—— came for a week ; thus my solitary hours are abridged ; we read together one or two sermons of Gisborne's every day, and a portion of general history in the evening. May I be rendered useful to these pleasing friends, by being enabled to make such remarks as may lead this young person to read common books with moral and religious advantage.

' My greatest loss in giving up the society of my distant friends is that I have fewer to stimulate me to the love of God. Lord, let this deficiency lead me to look more to the fountain.

' Long habits of vexation and disappointment, to which I am now inured, make ordinary trials light to me. Impatience has been one of my besetting evils ; it is still too ready to break out, even on occasions too small to record ; but it is less so than it was.

' Some painful occurrences. May we pity the errors, weaknesses, failings, and evil tempers of each other. Teach us, O Lord, to cultivate a spirit of Christian charity, and to bear with each other, especially as the days of age and imbecility advance.

' Let me be thankful that I have a comfortable evidence of growth in grace. I have lately heard of new enemies and of the malignity of old ones with composure ; and, I trust, with submission to the Divine will. Oh that I may be entirely delivered from the fear of man, and the desire of human praise !

' I was tempted to a piece of levity, of which I have rarely been guilty ; in writing a loyal paper I had approached too near to a parody on the Church Catechism. I am thankful that I felt my error, and altered the piece, even to its injury, to avoid giving offence to the serious, or any example of lightness to the vain.

' My religious reading has been much abridged, but I have in general kept up my hour of reflection at the close of the day ; a retirement I much enjoy and labour to secure. If religion has lost ground in my heart lately, a day or two of pain, through grace, may help to restore it. I had this morning in bed more comfortable intercourse with my Maker than of late.

' *Sunday, January* 15.—Ill-health detains me from church. Have been awakened to-day to more than usual fervour in prayer, in which I have been lately so dead. God grant there may not be more servile fear than filial love in it. O Lord, I have not loved Thee as I ought, and therefore I have not served Thee devotedly. I know not how much unbelief may be at the root of all this deadness. The Misses S—— here for some days —a painful breach healed—no misunderstanding ought to subsist for a day between Christian friends ; life is too short, peace too precious ; we must " bear one another's burdens." Christ bore *all* ours.

' Lord, look upon Cheddar—suffer not the work begun there to fail.

' Lord, I come to Thee persuaded that all Thy ways are perfect wisdom, and all Thy dispensations perfect goodness.

' *Sunday, January* 22.—After a week of too much worldliness, my mind has somewhat recovered its tone in devout prayer in the night. I have also to-day prayed with more affection. I have endeavoured to check my own spirit, by placing death before my eyes, and carefully reading Doddridge's last chapter—the dying scene. When I read, the impression is strong, and my mind serious ; but when the book is closed, the heart grows cold, and the world rushes in. Some worldly trials in the week have given me less vexation than usual, but that may be, not because my resignation is greater, but my animal spirits better.

' *January* 25.—I bless God for the holy example my friend N—— is giving of the power of religion—under tedious, painful, and dangerous disease —she is divinely supported—her children and servants are grown serious through her means ; Divine grace has made her to be willing to die, and resign her numerous children into the hands of her heavenly Parent.

' *Sunday, February* 19.—How uncertain are all sublunary things ! Just as the delay of the invasion was lulling the country into a false peace, it has pleased God to afflict us with an awful visitation—the sudden and alarming illness of the King. Into what new calamities may this sad event plunge this unthinking nation ! O Lord, in mercy remember us ! Avert, if Thou seest fit, this heavy stroke. Though we have rebelled against Thee, and our national iniquities cry aloud against us, yet do Thou spare us, or do Thou overrule this event to his everlasting salvation and for the public good : comfort and bless the royal sufferer, support and strengthen him under every trial, especially under the last great conflict. Sanctify it to his family, and grant that it may bring us all to a more serious temper, to a closer personal apprehension of the vanity of life, and a constant preparation for another world.

' *February* 28.—Our Bath house is sold. I am thankful for an event which fixes us to this place for the short remainder of life, without the turmoil, care, and expense of a divided dwelling and bustling town. Lord, grant that this may prove a blessing to us all, and draw us nearer to Thee. Make us thankful that our own lot is fallen in so pleasant a place—that we have a goodly heritage ; but let us not take up with so poor a portion as this life, or anything in it.

' *March* 7.—My diary is here interrupted, and may be so for a long time; the idea has been suggested to me to write a pamphlet on the education of the princess. I am unequal to it, yet they tell me it is a duty to attempt it ; I feel reluctant, but no irksomeness in the task should prevent me, if I dared hope I could do any good. Lord, if it be fit that I should undertake it, do Thou strengthen me for the work ; fill me with a holy boldness, with prudence and wisdom ; and if I really set about it, let Thy blessing, without which all is nothing, attend it. Have been reading the lives of Pascal, Cranmer, Hall. Few things are so profitable or so pleasant as the lives of eminent and holy men: the last is not impressively written—does not enter into those domestic details so interesting in the lives of good men. Cranmer seems faithfully delineated by Gilpin, and is of all characters the most interesting to me ; partly from a corresponding weakness : but a more religious use might have been made of it by Gilpin.

' *March* 12.—A visit at last from Mrs. ——, ardent, amiable, pious. I am humbled at her assuring me that my writings have been the honoured instruments of bringing her to the knowledge of the truth ; for, alas ! how little power have they on my own heart and life !

CHAPTER XV.

THERE remains little more to tell of the life and work of Mrs. Hannah More. The health and strength of all the five sisters were declining, and all suffered more or less during the years which followed their removal to Barley Wood. They were now all of them between the ages of seventy and eighty, and all their lives had been spent in incessant activity of mind and body. Even now none of them were idle, and Mrs. Hannah More and Mrs. Patty More continued their work in the villages of Mendip, superintending and planning, when they were no longer able themselves to teach in the schools.

The subject which seems to have engaged the mind of Hannah More at this time, and to which her last energies were given, was that of the moral life of Christians. A reaction against the dead forms of the past century had set in, and this 'lady of two centuries' saw now in the revival of doctrinal teaching, of appeals to the emotions, and efforts to awaken zeal, that there was danger lest the commands of God and the principles of external life laid down in the life and teaching of Christ should be overlooked, or held as secondary to orthodoxy of creed and warmth of feeling.

Her first work on this subject she called 'Practical Piety.'

10—2

Religion, she shows, was intended not for exceptional persons, but for the world at large ; it was to be the leaven working through all things, having to do with all life at every point. The common mistakes of the older ' moralists,' who separate morality from religion, and of the new ' professors,' who separate religion from morality, are both exposed, so that the work is just the blending of the foremost truths of both the eighteenth and nineteenth centuries in regard to religion. A good chapter, useful in every age, is the chapter on ' periodical religion,' in which the alternations of carelessness and repentance, alarm and indifference, severe renunciation and indulgence, are strikingly shown in all their emptiness and unfruitfulness.

' Practical Piety' was followed by ' Christian Morals,' and later still by ' Moral Sketches.' The last was written when she was in her seventy-fifth year, and bears on the surface some of the marks of age in its tone of plaintive anxiety respecting the special evils arising out of the newer time ; but here she still rises into ardent sympathy with all the best life of the coming days, with the breaking down of those barriers that shut off the lower classes from light and knowledge, and with the more tender love and concern which admitted the claims of every individual to help and protection. All these books are written with vigour, and with the thorough sound sense which was a special characteristic of Hannah More to the last.

The five sisters had up to this time lived in unbroken love and constant intercourse, ever since they had set out to seek their fortunes together, nearly sixty years before, in the school in Bristol ; but soon after the publication of ' Christian Morals,' the first of the band was taken from their pleasant home at

Barley Wood to her Father's house above. The eldest sister, on whose sense and energy the younger ones had all depended in the early days of their life together, was the first to leave them. A gradual decline of strength brought her life to a close on Easter Sunday, 1813. Hannah More writes of her: 'My dear eldest sister is escaped from this world of sorrow, and is, I humbly trust, through the mercy of her God and the merits of her Saviour, translated to a world of peace, where there will be neither sin, sorrow, nor separation. Her desire to be gone was great. I thought it something blessed to die on Easter Sunday, to descend to the grave on the day when Jesus triumphed over it.'

Three years later Mrs. Betty More, the second sister, was taken from them. She had been the housekeeper of the family, and her kindness and care were much missed by the remaining sisters. At that time Mrs. Sally More was in a dangerous state from dropsy, but, as Hannah More writes, 'still retains all the spirit and vivacity of her youth,' often cheering her sisters by the liveliness that had long ago so charmed Dr. Johnson. Mrs. Patty More, Hannah More's fellow-worker in the Mendip villages, was suffering from a liver complaint, and in a very declining state.

Six months afterwards Mrs. Sally More's sufferings, so bravely borne, were ended. To the last she maintained the same playful brightness and courageous endurance of pain which she had shown all through her illness. 'This sprightly, gay-tempered creature,' says Hannah More, 'whose vivacity age had not tamed, exhibited the most edifying spectacle I ever beheld. I cannot do justice to her humility, her patience, her submission. It was *more* than resignation, it was a sort of spiritual triumph over the sufferings of her tormented body.

On one occasion one of her sisters said to her, 'Poor Sally! you are in dreadful pain.' She answered, 'I am indeed, but it is all well.'

A friend who attended her all through her last illness, thus writes :

'While still so well as to be able, in some degree, to pursue her usual sedentary employments, she gave a striking proof how entirely she was withdrawing her mind from the things of this world, by refusing to have her chair placed near the bow-window, from whence she could enjoy the sight of those plants and flowers which it had been her constant amusement and delight to cultivate, but from which she now turned with an expression of the most entire indifference.

'At length it became impossible for her any longer to support a sitting position, and just before she was assisted upstairs for the last time, she threw a look all around her, evidently taking a mental farewell of the scene to which she had been so long accustomed, with an expression which, though she uttered no word, was full of solemn meaning. The extremity and constancy of her sufferings at length deprived her of the power of attending to a chain of reading which had hitherto been her chief delight and solace. To supply in some measure this loss, her sisters used to repeat from time to time a few detached texts, in which she would constantly join with the greatest fervour. During the last two years of her life more especially, she had been so diligent and constant a reader of the Scriptures, as well as of other devotional books, that her mind had become completely imbued with them ; and it was very remarkable, that in the moments of her sharpest pain, her attention was instantly excited, and her mind visibly comforted, if any bystander recited a verse from the Scripture, or a short prayer, in which, even when unable to speak, she joined with deep fervour.

'One day, after she had lain some time in an almost insensible state, a friend tried her with a few texts of Scripture ; she suddenly burst forth, "Can anything be finer than that? it quite makes one's face shine !" Towards the latter part of her illness she asked one day to have a little girl in whom she was interested brought to her. She could only deliver herself in short sentences, but her words were, " God bless thee, my dear child ; love God ; serve God ; love to pray to God more than to do any other thing." One night she complained of too much light, adding that "the smallest light was enough to die by." Mrs. H. More asked her if she had comfort in her mind? "Yes," she replied, "I have no uncomfort at all." She was then asked if she knew some friend that was in the room. "Oh yes!" she answered; "I know everybody and remember everything." "Poor dear soul," said one of her attendants, "she remembers her sufferings too!" "No," she answered, in a tone of the most affecting resignation; "I do not think of them." When she was supposed to be very near her last hour, on her medical attendant wishing her good morning, she raised her hands in a holy transport, exclaiming, "Oh for the glorious morning of the resurrection!—but there are some grey clouds between!" She then blessed him with all his family, and exhorted him to love God, and to take care of his soul. "Oh," she exclaimed, "if this should be the blessed hour of my deliverance, may I die the death of the righteous, and may my last thoughts be thoughts of faithfulness!" The following day she awoke suddenly out of a tranquil sleep, crying out in a rapture, "Blessing, and honour, and glory, and power, be unto the Lamb—Hallelujah!" Another morning, when she was imagined to be in the very act of dying, recovering herself a little, she murmured out, "When shall I come to these things—grace—mercy—peace!" She then asked for a little cold water, and turning her head towards a nurse who was attending her, "Do you know who it was that said, 'A cup of cold water given in My name'?"

'Again, in the intervals between her wanderings and the extremity of pain, she exclaimed incessantly, "Oh, the blood of Christ! He died for me! God was made man! May His blood be shed on me!" "Lord, let the light of Thy countenance shine upon me." "When shall I appear before God?" And then half bewildered again, she cried out earnestly to her sister, "Patty, *do* love the blessed God! Lord, shield me with the wings of Thy love." After a little interval, she said to Mrs. H. More, "I hope I have had all my stripes; Lord, I am ready—finish the work!" On awaking in the afternoon, she again poured forth this ejaculation, "Lord, look down upon me with the light of Thy salvation; let Thy Holy Spirit shine upon me. Look, O Lord! upon Thy afflicted servant." When somebody present said to her, "The Lord will release you, and take you out of your pain," she seemed to fear lest she had betrayed some impatience, and immediately answered, "Aye, in His own good time." She then broke out into the Gloria Patri, and added, "Lord, look down upon a poor penitent, humble, contrite sinner."

'Nearly three days now passed, either in strong delirium, or total stupor, at the end of which time she became more composed, and, as at every other time, uttered no sentence in which supplication or praise was not mingled. Her chief cry on this day was for pardon and sanctification, and she charged her sisters to strive for the gift of the Holy Spirit. Her wanderings were frequent, but whether sensible or incoherent, calm or agitated, still the names of her God and her Saviour were constantly on her tongue.

'Her sister asked her if she knew her : she answered, "I know nobody but Christ." In the evening of her last day but one, though scarcely able to articulate, she murmured out to those who stood around her, "Talk of the cross—the precious cross—the King of love." On the morning of her blessed and quiet release from an earthly existence, though no longer able to swallow food, or discern any outward object, she was still enabled to give an evidence of the heavenly frame of her mind ; when a friend repeated to her that heart-sustaining assurance, "That the blood of Christ cleanseth from all sin," she pronounced with a devout motion of her hands and eyes, "cleanseth," and a moment after," Blessed Jesus !" and these were the last of her words that could be collected. It is scarcely necessary to repeat, after such a relation, that her whole conduct during her conflict with this last enemy was one uniform and uninterrupted display (when she was in possession of her faculties) of those fruits of the Spirit enumerated by the apostle, " Love, peace, meekness, long-suffering, faith :" and it only remains for us to pray that our latter end may be like hers.'

The loss of this sister, whose bright intelligence and gaiety of heart made her the sunshine of the home, was deeply felt by Mrs. Hannah More and her sister Patty. They were both suffering, too, from bad health and declining strength ; but for two more years it pleased God to spare them as companions to one another. They had toiled and rejoiced together in their work in the Mendip villages, and the parting, when it came at last, was very hard to bear. Mr. and Mrs. Wilberforce had been staying in the house, and Mrs. Patty More had exerted herself to go with them to Cheddar and some of the other villages. In the night she was seized with violent inflammation, and four days afterwards Mrs. Hannah More was left alone, and Mrs. Patty's long and very useful life was ended.

'I may now indeed say,' writes the solitary survivor of this band of distinguished sisters, 'my house is left unto me desolate. I bless my heavenly Father, however, that He has not left me without consolation and support. And when I reflect on *her* immense gain, I am ashamed to dwell so much on my own loss. I find not one reason to murmur, but many for thanksgivings. She was enabled, after a life of devotedness to God, to bear her dying testimony to His faithfulness and truth. I feel thankful that she is removed from a world of pain and suffering, of sin and sorrow, to that blessed state purchased for her by Him who loved her and gave Himself for her; that she indeed sleeps in Jesus. Her last words were expressive of her strong Christian hope. When a friend pitied the excruciating pain she was suffering, she said, "Oh, I love my sufferings; they come from God, and I love everything that comes from Him." Shall I mourn such a death? And yet I cannot but mourn deeply. The remainder of my pilgrimage, however, must be short. My chief earthly support is removed, that I may lean more entirely on God. She is spared feeling for me what I now feel for her.'

The year following her sister's death, to all human appearance, she herself was on the point of departing. She aroused her household in the night-time, being seized with a suffocating obstruction on the chest. Her illness was very tedious, and it was expected to be her last. Even when the fear of an immediate dissolution was removed, it was not expected that she would survive during another winter. For herself, she did not seem to have any care or anxiety on the subject. 'I thank God,' she said to a clergyman who had been praying by her bedside, ' I have not the slightest anxiety whether to live or die. There is peace and safety at the foot of the cross. Blessed be His holy name, I am enabled to cast myself there, in a full, undivided, unqualified reliance on that blood that was shed upon it.' It pleased God yet to preserve her useful life for various years. In another bad attack on a future occasion, she then said : 'If I could determine for life or death by holding up my hand, I would not do it. . . . I seem to long as much for the holiness as the happiness of heaven ; it is such a blessed idea to be delivered from the possibility of sinning.' In reading the thirty-ninth psalm, when she came to the verse, ' Oh, spare me a little,' she broke short, saying : 'That part I will not repeat : it does not express my feelings.'

She recovered from these dangerous attacks so far as to be able once more to receive her multitudinous visitors, although much of the annals of the closing years of her life is occupied by the narrative of her dangerous illnesses and remarkable recoveries. She was hardly able to answer half her letters, but she did her best for her visitors. It was her system, on her first introduction to worldly characters, not immediately to press upon them the subject of religion, if it was likely that they would meet her more than once ; but if it was a single opportunity, she would try and come to the point at once. Many of her visitors brought her cheering news. One had met with one of her works in Iceland ; another told her that a Russian princess was translating some of her tracts into the Russian language ; and a third that some of her poems were being translated into the Cingalese tongue. Some of the best people in the world came to see her, using the word 'best' in its highest sense. At one time it is Mr. Wilberforce; at another time Dr. Chalmers comes; or it may be a bishop of the infant Episcopal Church of America; then it would be Mr. Jay, or perhaps her correspondent Mr. Foster; or it is Rowland Hill. 'I had been told so much of his oddities in the pulpit, that I was prepared for something amusingly absurd. But, as the phrase is, I reckoned without my host, or rather without my guest. As a proof that he takes good works largely into his notions of religion, when I asked him if it were true that he had vaccinated six thousand poor people with his own hand, his answer was, "Very near eight thousand."' Among her visitors there was one who was very remarkable—one who was considered the cleverest schoolboy and the cleverest undergraduate in England. Hannah More's piercing glance discovered her visitor's vast capabilities. She 'wished Tom was in Parliament, for then he would surpass them all.' She lived to see it. It was Thomas Babington Macaulay of whom she speaks, the future peer and historian.

For eight years she continued to live at Barley Wood, having generally some friend staying with her as a companion; and left as she was, the last of her family, yet she was no solitary stranded wreck, cast upon a desert shore, when all besides had gone down. Her old friends of the eighteenth century had passed away, one of the last of them being Sir William Pepys, the 'Lælius' of her 'Bas Bleu,' who died in 1825, after a friendship with her of fifty years, and another, Mrs. Garrick, who lived to the age of a hundred; but Hannah More's heart was in the nineteenth century as well as in the past. She loved the people and the work which had succeeded to the old order of things, for she felt that, under the rule of God, the world was passing to a brighter and not a darker day, that there were hope and life around her, though hers were fading now.

Mrs. Hannah More had hoped to end her life at Barley Wood, the home which had become most dear to her, the purchase of her own toil, the object of her special taste, and from which the four sisters had passed away to their Father's house above ; but in her eighty-fourth year circumstances induced her to leave the much-loved spot. All her early life had unfitted her for attending in any way to the domestic management of a household, and since the sisters had lived together that part of their home arrangements had fallen to those most accustomed to it. After their deaths everything was left to the servants, and a thorough system of robbery and misconduct was carried on by them. It was some time before this was made known to Mrs. Hannah More, and then it was a kind friend who discovered to her what almost everyone around had long been conscious of. She felt her inability to contend with the household difficulties of keeping up a sufficient establishment for Barley Wood, and she resolved to sell the place, and to remove to Clifton, using her money for the service of God while she still lived, instead of waiting till death made it useless to her. Still the trial was great, and as she left the house, she exclaimed, ' I am driven like Eve out of Paradise, but not like Eve by angels.'

Her new abode was on Windsor Terrace, Clifton, and she lived here for rather more than five years. With the exception of some loss of memory, Mrs. Hannah More retained the use of her mental powers till the close of her eighty-seventh year, taking still the deepest interest in public events of the time, and in the work being carried on in the Mendip villages ; but during the last year of her life she suffered much from inflammation of the lungs, and the inflammatory symptoms passed at times to the brain, disturbing the clearness of her intellectual powers. To the very last she retained sight and hearing unimpaired.

During her last illness there was the shining within of that clear light of utter trust in the love of God which gave such brightness to the even-tide of her sisters' lives. She talked much of the many mercies of God to her through her long life, often making use of such expressions as 'God of light, God of love.' 'I know that my Redeemer liveth. Oh, the love of Christ, the love of Christ !' 'It is glorious to die to go to heaven—think what *that* is !'

The fifty-first psalm was always on her lips : 'Create in me a clean heart, O God ; renew a right spirit within me. Cast me not away from Thy presence, and take not Thy Holy Spirit from me.' 'I love you, my dear child, with fervency,' she said to the lady who was with her. 'It will be pleasant to you twenty years hence to remember that I said this on my death-bed.' When she was asked if anything could be done to make her more comfortable, she answered, 'Nothing but love me, and forgive me when I am impatient. I hope my temper is not peevish or troublesome.' When they answered that it was the temper of an angel, she replied, 'Oh no, not of an angel, but of a very highly favoured servant of the Lord, my Saviour.' Her servant proposed to read a chapter to her, and she said, 'What are you going to read ?' and upon being told the 'resurrection of Christ,' she said, 'If we meet at His feet we shall be equal.' And when an attendant was repeating some psalms and hymns, she said, 'You cannot have your mind too much stored with these things ; when you get old or in solitude they will supply you with comfort.' Again, to

a friend, ' To go to heaven, think what *that* is ! to go to my
Saviour who died that I might live.   Lord, humble me;
subdue every evil temper in me.   May we meet in a robe of
glory ! through Christ's merits alone can we be saved !   Look
down, O Lord, upon Thy unworthy servant with eyes of compassion. . . . It pleases God to afflict me, not for His pleasure, but to do me good, to make me humble and thankful ;
Lord, I believe; I *do* believe with all the powers of my weak,
sinful heart.   Lord Jesus, look down upon me from Thy
holy habitation ; strengthen my face and quicken me in my
preparation.   Support me in that trying hour when I most
need it ; it is a glorious thing to die !'   And when some one
mentioned to her the good deeds which she had wrought, she
answered, ' Talk not so vainly ; I utterly cast them from me,
and fall low at the foot of the cross.'

'On Friday the 6th of December, 1833,' writes a friend,
' we offered up the morning family devotion by her bedside :
she was silent, and apparently attentive, with her hands
devoutly lifted up.   From eight in the evening of this day
till nearly nine I sat watching her.   Her face was smooth
and glowing.   There was an unusual brightness in its expression.   She smiled, and endeavouring to raise herself a little
from her pillow, she reached out her arms as if catching at
something, and while making this effort she once called
"Patty," the name of her last and dearest sister, very plainly,
and exclaimed, "Joy."

'In this state of quietness and inward peace she remained
for about an hour.   At half-past nine o'clock, Dr. Carrick
came.   The pulse had become extremely quick and weak.   At
about ten, the symptoms of speedy departure could not be
doubted.   She fell into a dozing sleep, and slight convulsions

succeeded, which seemed to be attended with no pain. She
breathed softly, and looked serene. The pulse became fainter
and fainter, and as quick as lightning. It was almost extinct
from twelve o'clock, when the whole frame was very serene.
With the exception of a sigh or a groan, there was nothing
but the gentle breathing of infant sleep. Contrary to expectation, she survived the night. She continued till ten minutes
after one, when I saw the last gentle breath escape ; and one
more was added " to that multitude which no man can
number, who sing the praises of God and of the Lamb for
ever and ever." '

Few indeed among ' honourable women ' have spent such
a useful and beneficent career. Her writings, which, generally
speaking, are more the offspring of sound sense and careful
culture than genius and originality, will probably obtain a
less permanent value than her contemporaries expected. But
the influence which they had in her own lifetime was immense,
and it would be difficult to gauge the length and the breadth
of the good which they accomplished. To this must be added
the practical and religious benefits diffused by this remarkable
sisterhood far and wide throughout the neighbourhood in
which they resided. Moreover, the life of Hannah More was
in beautiful harmony with her words of wisdom and works of
mercy ; her example is fraught with influence, and the record
of her days with instruction.

> ' Only the actions of the just,
> Smell sweet and blossom in the dust.'

Hannah More's life, read aright, is full of meaning. She
was no mere spoiled child of a literary circle, no mere trite
moralist of the last century, no mere narrow religionist of a
doctrinal clique ; and yet she has been too much regarded by

a later generation as one or all of these. She sympathized
with the literary life of her own time such as she found it;
she felt the good sense of the practical morality of the
English people, especially as standing in relief against
German sentimentalism and French license; and she warmly
received those truths brought into prominence by the evan-
gelical revival. She stands thus before us as an illustration
of how much pure religion, sound morality, and wide culture
are all needed rightly to understand our age, and to do true
work for God in it. It was this combination of forces, too
often disunited, which gave her so much influence and
strength, and which formed the ground of her steadfast,
cheerful faith in God's rule :

> ' That God which ever lives and loves,
>   One God, one law, one element,
>   And one far-off Divine event,
> To which the whole creation moves.'

THE END.

BILLING AND SONS, PRINTERS, GUILDFORD AND LONDON.